STRANGER THINGS

RUNAWAY MAX

Brenna Yovanoff

EMBER

Cover and interior art used under license from Shutterstock.com
Cover art copyright © 2021 by Netflix, Inc.
Text copyright © 2021 by Netflix, Inc.

Ember and the E colophon are registered trademarks of Penguin Random House LLC.

Stranger Things and all related titles, characters, and logos are trademarks of Netflix, Inc. Created by the Duffer Brothers.

Visit us on the Web! GetUnderlined.com

Educators and librarians, for a variety of teaching tools, visit us at RHTeachersLibrarians.com

Library of Congress Cataloging-in-Publication Data is available upon request.

ISBN 978-0-593-17951-2 (paperback)

Printed in the United States of America
10 9 8 7 6 5 4 3 2
First Ember Edition 2021

For the daring girls and the hopeful boys

And for V., my strangest thing

PROLOGUE

The floor of the San Diego bus station was mostly cigarette butts. A million years ago, the building had probably been fancy, like Grand Central or those huge places you see in movies. But now it just looked gray all over, like a warehouse full of crumpled band flyers and winos.

It was almost midnight, but the lobby was crowded. Next to me, a wall of storage lockers ran all the way down to the end. One of the lockers was leaking a little, like something had spilled inside and was dripping out onto the floor. It was sticking to my shoes.

There were vending machines on the other side of the lobby, and there was a bar over in the corner, where a bunch of skinny, stubbly men sat smoking into ashtrays, hunched over their beers like goblins. The smoke made the air look hazy and weird.

I hurried along, close to the lockers, keeping my chin down and trying not to look obvious. Back at my house, when I'd imagined this scene, I'd been pretty sure I'd be able to blend into the crowd, no problem. But now that I was here, it was harder than I'd pictured. I'd been counting on the chaos and the size to cover me. It was a *bus* station, after all. I didn't figure I'd be the only one here who was still too young to drive.

On my street or at school, I was easy to overlook—twelve years old and average height, average shape and face and clothes. Average everything except for my hair, which was long and red and the brightest thing about me. I yanked it into a ponytail and tried to walk like I knew where I was going. I should have brought a hat.

Over at the ticket windows, a couple of older girls in green eyeshadow and rubber miniskirts were arguing with the guy behind the glass. Their hair was teased up so high it looked like cotton candy.

"C'mon, man," said one of them. She was shaking her purse upside down on the window ledge, counting out quarters. "Can't you cut me a break? I'm barely short. Only a buck fifty."

The guy looked sarcastic and bored in his ratty Hawaiian shirt. "Does this look like a charity? No fare, no ticket."

I reached into the pocket of my warm-up jacket and ran my fingers over my own ticket. Economy from San Diego to LA. I'd paid for it with a twenty from my mom's jewelry box and the guy had barely looked at me.

I walked faster, sticking close to the wall with my skateboard under my arm. For a second, I thought how badass it would be to set it down and go zooming between the benches. But I didn't. One wrong move and even a bunch of late-night dirtbags were going to notice I wasn't supposed to be here.

I was almost to the end of the lobby when a nervous ripple went through the crowd behind me. I turned around. Two guys in tan uniforms were standing by the vending machines, looking out over the sea of faces. Even from across the station, I could catch the glint of their badges. Cops.

The tall one had fast, pale eyes and long, skinny arms like a spider. He was pacing up and down between the benches in that way cops always do. It's a slow, official walk that says *I might be a creepy string bean, but I'm the one with the badge and the gun.* It reminded me of my stepdad.

If I could get to the end of the lobby, I could slip out to the depot where the buses pulled up. I'd slide into the crowd and disappear.

The scuzzy guys at the bar hunched lower over their beers. One of them mashed out his cigarette, then gave the cops a long, nasty stare and spit on the floor between his feet. The girls at the ticket window had stopped arguing with the cashier. They were acting really interested in their press-on nails, but looked plenty nervous about Officer String Bean. Maybe they had the same kind of stepdads I did.

The cops waded out into the middle of the lobby and were squinting around the bus station like they were looking for something. A lost kid, maybe. A bunch of delinquents up to no good.

Or a runaway.

I ducked my head and got ready to blend in. I was just about to step out into the terminal when someone cleared his throat and a big, heavy hand closed around my arm. I turned and looked up into the looming face of a third cop.

He smiled a bored, flat smile, all teeth. "Maxine Mayfield? I'm going to need you to come with me." His face was hard and craggy, and he looked like he'd said the same thing to different kids about a hundred times. "You've got people at home worried sick about you."

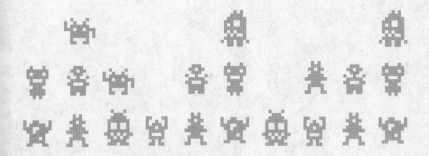

CHAPTER ONE

The sky was so low it seemed to be sitting right on top of downtown Hawkins. The world whipped past me as I clattered along the sidewalk. I skated faster, listening to the wheels whispering on concrete, then thudding over the cracks. It was a chilly afternoon, and the cold made my ears hurt. It had been chilly every day since we'd rolled into town three days ago.

I kept looking up, expecting to see the bright sky of San Diego. But here, everything was pale and gray, and even when it wasn't overcast, the sky looked colorless. Hawkins, Indiana: home of low gray clouds and quilted jackets and winter.

Home of . . . me.

Main Street was all tricked out for Halloween, with storefronts full of grinning pumpkins. Fake spiderwebs and paper skeletons were taped in the windows of the supermarket. All down the block, lampposts were wrapped in black-and-orange streamers fluttering in the wind.

I'd spent the afternoon at the Palace Arcade, playing *Dig Dug* until I ran out of quarters. Because my mom didn't like me wasting money on video games, back home in California I'd mostly only gotten to play when I'd been with my dad. He'd take me to the bowling alley with him, or sometimes the laundry, which had *Pac-Man* and *Galaga*. And I sometimes hung out at the Joy Town Arcade at the mall, even though it was a total rip-off and full of metalheads in ratty jeans and leather jackets. They had *Pole Position,* though, which was better than any other racing game and had a steering wheel like you were actually driving.

The arcade in Hawkins was a big, low-roofed building with neon signs in the windows and a bright yellow awning (but under the colored lights and the paint, it was just aluminum siding). They had *Dragon's Lair* and *Donkey Kong,* and *Dig Dug,* which was my best game.

I'd been hanging out there all afternoon, running up the score on *Dig Dug,* but after I entered my name in the number-one spot and I didn't have any more quarters, I started to feel antsy, like I needed to move, so I left the arcade and skated downtown to take a tour of Hawkins.

I pushed myself faster, rattling past a diner and a hardware store, a Radio Shack, a movie theater. The theater was small, like it might only have one screen, but the front was glitzy and old-fashioned, with a big marquee that stuck out like a battleship covered in lights.

The only time I really liked to sit still was at the movies. The newest poster out front was for *The Terminator,* but I'd already seen it. The story was pretty good. This killer robot who looks like Arnold Schwarzenegger travels back in time from the future to kill this waitress named Sarah Connor. At first she just seems kind of normal, but she turns out to be a total badass. I liked it, even though it wasn't a real monster movie, but something about it also made me feel weirdly disappointed. None of the women I knew were anything like Sarah Connor.

I was zipping past the pawn shop now—past a furniture store, past a pizza place with a red-and-green-striped awning—when something small and dark darted across the sidewalk in front of me. In the gray afternoon light, it looked like a cat, and I just had time to think how weird that was, how you'd never see a cat in downtown San Diego, before my feet went out from under me.

I was used to wiping out, but still, that split second of a fall was always disorienting. When I lost my balance, it felt like the whole world had flipped over and skidded out from under me. I hit the ground so hard I felt the thump in my teeth.

I'd been skating since forever—since my best friend, Nate Walker, and his brother Silas took a trip to Venice Beach with their parents when we were in the third grade and came back all jazzed up on stories about the Z-Boys and the skate shops in Dogtown. I'd been skating since the day I found out about grip tape and Madrid boards and rode down Sunset Hill for the first time and learned what it felt like to go so fast your heart raced and your eyes watered.

The sidewalk was cold. For a second, I lay flat on my stomach, with a thudding hollow in my chest and pain zinging up my arms. My elbow had punched through the sleeve of my sweater and the palms of my hands felt raw and electric. The cat was long gone.

I had rolled over and was trying to sit up when a thin, dark-haired woman came hurrying out of one of the stores. It was almost as surprising as a cat in the business district. No one in California would have come running out just to see if I was okay, but this was Indiana. My mom had said that people would be nicer here.

The woman was already kneeling next to me on the concrete with big, nervous eyes. I was bleeding a little where my elbow had gone through my sleeve. My ears were ringing.

She leaned close, looking worried. "Oh, your arm, that must hurt." Then she looked up, staring into my face. "Do you scare easily?"

I just stared back. *No,* I wanted to say, and that was true in all kinds of ways. I wasn't scared of spiders or dogs. I could walk along the boardwalk alone in the dark or skateboard in the wash in flood season and never worry that a murderer was going to jump out at me or that a sudden deluge of water would come rushing down to drown me. And when my mom and my stepdad said we were moving to Indiana, I packed some socks and underwear and two pairs of jeans in my backpack and headed for the bus station alone to escape to LA. It was a total trip to ask a stranger if they got scared. Scared of *what*?

For a second I just sat in the middle of the sidewalk with my elbow stinging and my palms raw and gritty, squinting at her. "What?"

She reached out to brush gravel off my hands. Hers were thinner and tanner than mine, with dry, cracked knuckles and bitten fingernails. Next to them, mine looked pale, covered in freckles.

She was watching me in a quick, nervous way, like I was the one acting weird. "I just wondered if you scar easily. Sometimes fair skin does. You should put Bactine on that to keep it from getting infected."

"Oh." I shook my head. The palms of my hands still felt like they were full of tiny sparks. "No. I mean, I don't think so."

She leaned closer and was about to say something else when suddenly her eyes got even bigger and she froze. We both looked up as the air was split by the roar of an engine.

A swimming-pool-blue Camaro came bombing through the stoplight at Oak Street and snarled up to the curb. The woman whipped around to see what the trouble was, but I already knew.

My stepbrother, Billy, was leaning back in the driver's seat with his hand draped lazily on the wheel. I could hear the blare of his music through the closed windows.

Even from the sidewalk, I could see the light glinting off Billy's earring. He was watching me in the flat, empty way he always did—heavy-lidded, like I made him so bored he could barely stand it—but under that was a glittering edge of something dangerous. When he looked at me like that, my face wanted to flush bright red or crumple. I was used to how he looked at me, like I was something he wanted to scrape off him, but it always seemed worse when he did it in front of someone else—like this nice, nervous woman. She looked like someone's mom.

I scrubbed my stinging hands on the thighs of my jeans before bending down to get my board.

He let his head flop back, his mouth open. After a second, he leaned across the seat and rolled down the window.

The stereo thumped louder, Quiet Riot pounding out into the chilly air. "Get in."

• • •

Once, for two weeks back in April, I thought that Camaro was the coolest thing I'd ever seen. It had a long, hungry body like a shark, all sleek painted panels and sharp angles. It was the kind of car you could rob a bank in.

Billy Hargrove was fast and hard-edged, like the car. He had a faded denim jacket and a face like a movie star.

Back then, he wasn't Billy yet, just this hazy idea I had about what my life was going to be like. His dad, Neil, was going to marry my mom, and when we all moved in together, Billy was going to be my brother. I was excited to have a family again.

After the divorce, my dad had hightailed it to LA, so I mostly only saw him on second-rate holidays, or when he was down in San Diego for work and my mom couldn't think up a reason not to let me.

My mom was still around, of course, but in a thin, floaty way that was hard to get a hold on. She'd always been a little blurry around the edges, but once my dad was out of the picture, it got worse. It was kind of tragic how easily she disappeared into the personality of every guy she dated.

There was Donnie, who was on disability for his back and couldn't bend down to take out the trash. He made us Bisquick pancakes on the weekends and told terrible jokes, and then one day he ran off with a waitress from IHOP.

After Donnie, there was Vic from St. Louis, and Gus with one green eye and one blue one, and Ivan, who picked his teeth with a folding knife.

Neil was different. He drove a tan Ford pickup and his shirts were ironed and his mustache made him look like some kind of army sergeant or park ranger. And he wanted to marry my mom.

The other guys had been losers, but they were temporary losers, so I never really minded them. Some of them were goofy or friendly or funny, but after a while, the bad stuff always piled up. They were behind on their rent, or they'd total their cars, or they'd get drunk and wind up in county.

They always left, and if they didn't, my mom kicked them out. I wasn't heartbroken. Even the best ones were kind of embarrassing. None of them were cool like my dad, but mostly they were okay. Some of them were even nice.

Like I said, Neil was different.

She met him at the bank. She was a teller there, sitting behind a smudgy window, handing out deposit slips and giving lollipops to little kids. Neil was a guard, standing all day by the double doors. He said she looked like Sleeping Beauty sitting there behind the glass, or like an old-timey painting in a frame. The way he said it, the idea was supposed to sound romantic, but I couldn't see how. Sleeping Beauty was in a coma. Paintings in frames weren't interesting or exciting—they were just stuck there.

The first time she had him over for dinner, he brought flowers. None of the other ones had ever brought flowers. He told her the meat loaf was the best meat loaf he'd ever had, and she smiled and blushed and glanced sideways at him. I was glad she'd stopped crying over her last boyfriend—a carpet salesman with a comb-over and a wife he hadn't told her about.

A few weeks before school let out for the summer, Neil asked my mom to marry him. He bought her a ring and she gave him the extra key to the house. He showed up when he felt like it, bringing flowers or getting rid of throw pillows and pictures he didn't like, but he didn't come over after ten and he never spent the night. He was too much of a gentleman for that—*old-fashioned,* he said. He liked clean counters and family dinners. The little gold engagement ring made her happier than I'd seen her in a long time, and I tried to be happy for her.

Neil had told us he had a son in high school, but that was all he said about him. I figured he would be some preppie football type, or else maybe a younger copy of Neil. I wasn't picturing Billy.

The night we finally met him, Neil took us out to Fort Fun, which was a go-kart track near my house where the surf rats went with their girlfriends to eat funnel cakes and play air hockey and Skee-Ball. It was the kind of place that guys like Neil would never be caught dead in. Later, I figured out that he was trying to make us think he was fun.

Billy was late. Neil didn't say anything, but I could tell he was mad. He tried to act like everything was fine, but his fingers left dents in his foam Coke cup. My mom fidgeted with a paper napkin while we waited, wadding it up and then tearing it into little squares.

I pretended that maybe it was all a big scam and Neil didn't even have a son. It was the kind of thing that was always happening in horror movies—the guy made up a whole fake life and told everyone about his perfect house and his perfect family, but actually he lived in a basement, eating cats or something.

I didn't really think it was the truth, but I imagined it anyway, because it was better than watching him glare out at the parking lot every two minutes and then smile tightly at my mom.

The three of us were working our way through a game of mini golf when Billy finally showed up. We were on the tenth hole, standing in front of a painted windmill the size of a garden shed and trying to get the ball past the turning sails.

When the Camaro roared into the parking lot, the engine was so loud that everyone turned to look. He got out, letting the door slam shut behind him. He had on his jean jacket and engineer boots, and raddest of all, he had an earring. Some of the older boys at school wore boots and jean jackets, but none of them had an earring. With his mop of sprayed hair and his open shirt, he looked like the metalheads at the mall, or David Lee Roth or someone else famous.

He came over to us, cutting straight through the mini-golf course.

He stepped over a big plastic turtle and onto the fake green turf.

Neil watched with the tight, sour look he always did when something wasn't up to his standards. "You're late."

Billy just shrugged. He didn't look at his dad.

"Say hello to Maxine."

I wanted to tell Billy that wasn't my name—I hated when people called me Maxine—but I didn't. It wouldn't have mattered. Neil always called me that, no matter how many times I told him to stop.

Billy gave me this slow, cool nod, like we already knew each other, and I smiled, holding my putter by its sweaty rubber handle. I was thinking how much cooler this was going to make me. How jealous Nate and Silas would be. I was getting a brother, and it was going to change my life.

Later, the two of us hung out by the Skee-Ball stalls while Neil and my mom walked down along the boardwalk together. It was getting kind of annoying, how they were always all gooey at each other, but I fed quarters into the slot and tried to ignore it. She seemed really happy.

Skee-Ball was on a raised concrete deck above the go-kart track. From the railing, you could look down and watch the cars go zooming around in a figure eight.

Billy leaned his elbows on the railing with his hands hanging loose and casual in front of him and a cigarette balanced between his fingers. "Susan seems like a real buzzkill."

I shrugged. She was fussy and nervous and could be no fun sometimes, but she was my mom.

Billy looked out over the track. His eyelashes were long, like a girl's, and I saw for the first time how heavy his eyelids were. That was the thing that I would come to learn about Billy, though—he never really looked awake, except . . . sometimes. Sometimes his face went suddenly alert, and then you had no idea what he was going to do or what was going to happen next.

"So. Maxine." He said my name like some kind of joke. Like it wasn't really my name.

I tucked my hair behind my ears and tossed a ball into the corner cup for a hundred points. The machine under the coin slot whirred and spit out a paper chain of tickets. "Don't call me that. It's Max or nothing."

Billy glanced back at me. His face was slack. Then he smiled a sleepy smile. "Well. You've got a real mouth on you."

I shrugged. It wasn't the first time I'd heard that. "Only when people piss me off."

He laughed, and it was low and gravelly. "Mad Max. All right, then."

Out in the parking lot, the Camaro was sitting under a streetlight, so blue it looked like a creature from another world. Some kind of monster. I wanted to touch it.

Billy had turned away again. He was leaning on the rail with the cigarette in his hand, watching the go-karts as they zoomed along the tire-lined track.

I sent the last ball clunking into the one-hundred cup and took my tickets. "You want to race?"

Billy snorted and took a drag off the cigarette. "Why would I want to screw around with some little go-kart when I know how to drive?"

"I know how to drive too," I said, even though it wasn't exactly true. My dad had taught me how to use the clutch once in the parking lot at Jack in the Box.

Billy didn't even blink. He tipped his head back and blew out a plume of smoke. "Sure you do," he said. He looked blank and bored under the flashing neon lights, but he sounded almost friendly.

"I *do.* As soon as I'm sixteen, I'm going to get a Barracuda and drive all the way up the coast."

"A 'Cuda, huh? That's a lot of horsepower for a little kid."

"So? I can handle it. I bet I could even drive your car."

Billy stepped closer and leaned down so he was staring right into my face. He smelled sharp and dangerous, like hair stuff and cigarettes. He was still smiling.

"Max," he said in a sly, singsong voice. "If you think you're getting anywhere near my car, you are extremely mistaken." But he was smiling when he said it. He laughed again, pinching the end of his cigarette and tossing it away. His eyes were bright.

And I'd figured it was all a big goof, because it was just how guys like that talked. The slackers and the lowlifes my dad knew—all the ones who hung out at the Black Door Lounge down the street from his apartment in East

Hollywood. When they made jokes about Sam Mayfield's daredevil daughter or teased me about boys, they were only playing.

Billy was looming over me, studying my face. "You're just a kid," he said again. "But I guess even kids can tell a bitchin' ride when they see one, right?"

"Sure," I said.

And I'd actually been dumb enough to believe that this was the start of something good. That the Hargroves were here to make everything better—or at least okay. That this was family.

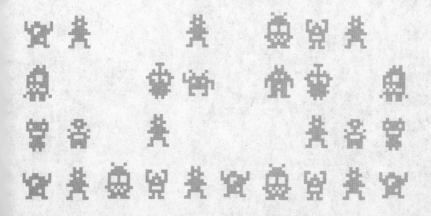

CHAPTER TWO

My first day at Hawkins Middle School was a Tuesday, more than a month after the school year had already started. My mom hadn't made us go the day before because they didn't have all our records yet. But that morning, she stuck her head into my room and told me to get up.

All my stuff was still in boxes, and I thought she was going to make me unpack, but instead, she just smiled thinly and said it was time for school. I had an idea that maybe having Billy around all the time was starting to make her a little crazy. Or maybe she finally just noticed that I'd spent three days at the arcade. I would have spent a fourth there, but I couldn't skip school forever, and I was out of money anyway.

After breakfast, I got my backpack and my board and followed Billy out the door.

The Camaro smelled the way it always did—like hairspray and cigarettes. Billy slid into the driver's seat and gunned the engine. The car roared awake with a ragged snarl, and then we were tearing down the two-lane farm road into town, past woods and fields and a whole lot of cows.

In the driver's seat, Billy stared straight ahead. "God, this place sucks. I bet you're already planning your next jailbreak, right?"

I looked out the passenger window with my chin in my hand. "No."

My mom'd nearly had an embolism when the cops had brought me home from the San Diego bus station. She kept going on and on about how bad I'd scared them, and how dangerous it was to just go running off to god knew where, but she was totally missing the point. I hadn't been running off to god knew where, I'd been going to LA to see my dad. To my mom, though, that was pretty much the same thing.

Ever since they split up, my dad had been living in this crappy little apartment in East Hollywood with matted carpet and windows so dirty they made everything look like it was underwater.

He sunburned even more easily than I did—Black Irish, with hair so dark it looked dyed and skin you could see the veins through. He knew science and math and all the

answers to the Sunday crossword puzzle, and could pick a
Master Lock padlock with just a paper clip and a piece of
Coke can.

My mom hated it when I went to stay with him. She
worried about everything—muggers and traffic accidents
and whether or not I'd have a bedtime. Even back when
they'd gotten along, he was always giving her fits just by letting me do things that she wouldn't. It wasn't hard to make
my mom freak out, but the things she worried about with
him weren't even major. It wasn't like he was taking me to
dog fights—he was just letting me light off Black Cats or
showing me how to use his drill to make a derby car out of
roller skates and orange crates.

After the divorce, my mom got even more nervous, and
my dad got more careless. When I came home with a torn
jacket or a new scrape on my knee, she would practically
go into hysterics. I didn't tell her about the parking lot at
Jack in the Box and him teaching me to drive his ratty old
Impala.

When I told her about weekends at my dad's, it was easy
to leave out the parts she wouldn't like. How he was always
late to meet me at the bus station, or how he sometimes
passed out in front of the TV. On weekends, he liked to
drive up to the racetrack, and I'd sit on a vinyl stool next to
him and eat peanuts and watch the horses.

Moving in with him wouldn't have been the worst thing
in the world. LA was cool. They had punk clubs and Oki
Dog and all-girl skater gangs. I'd miss my friends, but things

had gotten weird with them that summer. I wasn't even sure it mattered anymore.

I'd never really thought about San Diego one way or another until I found out we were leaving. Neil and my mom sat us down in the living room and told us they'd decided that we were moving to Indiana, but that was a lie. Neil had decided. My mom just nodded and smiled and went along with it.

Billy was the one who lost it. He blasted his music and slammed around the house and stopped showing up for dinner.

I just decided I wasn't going.

My escape was short-lived, though. The police brought me home, and I packed all my stuff in ten cardboard liquor boxes and watched the movers stack them in the back of a rental truck. And now we were here in Hawkins.

The whole place was smaller than I'd pictured, but kind of sweet, too. It might be okay. The little downtown was small and shabby, but at least they decorated for Halloween. And they had an arcade. How bad could a place be if it had an arcade?

Next to me, Billy was staring at the road ahead like it offended him.

• • •

Hawkins Middle was a long brick building across the parking lot from the high school. It was plain and sturdy, more like a county jail than a school. My mom had told Billy to drop me off and then come in with me and make sure they had all my stuff, but he just blew past the front entrance and gunned it up to the high school parking lot.

"Hey!" I stared at him and banged my hand on the dashboard. "You're supposed to drop me off."

Billy rolled his head sideways to look at me. "But I don't want to, Max. They're not paying me to babysit you. If you don't like it, maybe tomorrow you can walk."

I didn't answer, just grabbed my board and my schoolbag. When I got out of the car, I didn't look back.

The main office was easy to find, down a little hall to one side of the front doors.

The woman behind the counter had a shiny old-fashioned blouse. When I told her why I was there, she looked at me like I was some kind of strange new creature.

Finally she turned and called back to another lady who was digging through a filing cabinet. "Doris, do we have a class schedule for Mayfield?"

The second lady put down her folders and came up to the counter. "What do you need a class schedule in the middle of the semester for?" she said, like I'd confused her.

I didn't answer, just sighed and made my eyes wide and impatient. It was a look my mom couldn't stand. She said it was because I was making things harder for myself, but I could tell it made her feel embarrassed, like she had to apologize for me. I wasn't being nice.

I was almost sure the office ladies would make me stow

my skateboard. In Cali, the rule had been that you had to keep it in your locker, but here no one said anything about it. Maybe they didn't even have a rule for skateboards. Maybe they'd never seen one.

My first class was science, and I got there after the bell.

Even though everyone was already seated, the room had a lot of empty desks, like the class was supposed to be bigger. I knew it was just because the classroom was big and Hawkins was small, but the empty places made it seem like the part in a story where everyone goes off to fight a monster and they don't all come back.

The teacher made me stand at the front of the room while he introduced me. It's so annoying how certain kinds of grown-ups always call you by your full name, like you've done something wrong. When I corrected him, some of the girls giggled or whispered, but the boys only stared.

The rest of the morning was even worse, like the school was trying to prove to me exactly how much I didn't belong there. In history, everyone else was working on their semester projects. The teacher, Mr. Rogan, had me do a photocopied worksheet while everyone else pushed their desks together in threes and fours, and then he didn't even remember to make me hand it in.

I hadn't had to actually make friends since I was a little kid. I'd never figured out how to talk to other girls. Back home, they always acted weirded out over how I didn't care about press-on nails and perms, or how when I watched monster movies, I didn't do it just to squeal and scream. Every day during summer, they'd lie out by the pool and cover each other's shoulders with baby oil and talk about boys. I wasn't interested in burning myself up trying to get a tan, and I knew actual boys and pretty much none of them were worth swooning over.

This past weekend my mom had been on a homemaker kick, unpacking everything, then folding and ironing it. Finally, she ran out of her own clothes, and I caught her in my room, going through the boxes. That morning, she'd gotten out the floppy Esprit cardigan she bought me last year at Fashion Barn and put it on my bed. The cardigan was pastel striped, with big plastic buttons. I'd never worn it in my life. I stood looking at it, trying to figure out exactly what she wanted. I was already dressed in jeans and a pullover like I wore every day.

"What's that for?" I said. I knew I should want to make her happy, but I wasn't about to show up to my first day at a new school dressed as someone else.

She smiled weakly. "It's your first day. I thought you might like to wear something a little special."

"Why?"

Her smile faded and she looked away, fiddling with the sleeve of the cardigan. "Oh, I don't know. It just seems like a waste, you know? You're so pretty, but you never dress up or try to look nice."

The idea that I needed to dress up for Hawkins was so

idiotic I almost laughed. I didn't feel very pretty, and I definitely wasn't nice.

At lunch, I ate beef jerky and pretzels out of a paper bag and sat alone on the cracked concrete steps by the gym. We still hadn't unpacked the kitchen, and we needed to go grocery shopping. For the first time since leaving San Diego, I really let myself feel the hollow in my chest. It took a minute to recognize it. *Loneliness.*

At home I'd had Ben Voss, Eddie Harris, and Nate. We spent summers and afternoons after school skating, or else building forts in the dry creek behind my house.

And even after he moved to LA, I'd had my dad. He was full of ideas and knew how to make it feel like he was with me even when he wasn't. He'd always gotten really excited about puzzles—spy kits, secret codes, dead drops. It was the solving that he liked. When I was little, before he moved to LA, he used to hide notes for me in my homework. I'd be working on a history report or flipping through my language arts book, and there between the pages would be a little square of folded paper with a message in code, or a puzzle he'd made using circles and triangles, or words that sounded alike but were spelled different.

I thought it was cool, but it drove my mom nuts. She could never seem to get over how mad she was that he could be that smart and that good at things but still work nights at the bail bond place, or sometimes not work at all. He wasn't a nine-to-five person, though. The jobs he did were mostly under-the-table, and after the divorce, he kind of stopped pretending it had been any other way. He slept late and spent his nights hustling pool or making fake IDs. The ways he made money embarrassed my mom, but they made sense to me. I got how it was to know you were supposed to be following the rules but still feel so spun up you thought you were going to explode. The only thing was to hold still and wait it out and as soon as the bell rang, go tearing out the door and down the street in a whoosh of air.

Over by the four-square grid, a little pack of girls was standing in a circle, lazily bouncing the rubber four-square ball between them. They were all the kind of girl my mom probably wished I'd turn into, in corduroy jumpers and plaid skirts down to their shins. They didn't even wear wet n wild nail polish or tease their bangs. Two of them were wearing cardigans, and all I could think was how relieved my mom would be to know she'd been right after all.

For a second, I thought about going over to them, but what was I supposed to say? I could never figure out the right things to say to make some girl in a flannel skirt be my friend. How pathetic.

I spent the rest of the lunch period cruising back and forth over the sloping pavement behind the school. I was rattling down the hill for the third time when I got a weird, twitchy feeling, like being in a spotlight.

There was a group of boys over by the gate to the football field. They were all clustered together behind the chain-link fence. Watching me.

I wasn't sure, but I thought I recognized them from first period. They were half-hidden behind the fence, and I realized they were spying on me, but they weren't being very slick about it. One of them whispered something, and they all leaned closer, as if I couldn't see them standing there.

All day, I'd been feeling off balance, like time was moving much too slow. I needed to prove something, or maybe just make up for the fact that besides my teachers and the ladies in the office, no one had talked to me all day.

I took out the crumpled history assignment and scrawled a message on the back, not a puzzle, not in code. In plain English, telling them to stay away from me. I wrote fast and slanted, but I wasn't even sure that I meant it. If I really wanted to be left alone, maybe I wouldn't have written anything at all.

I threw the note in the trash and walked inside, the doors sighing shut behind me.

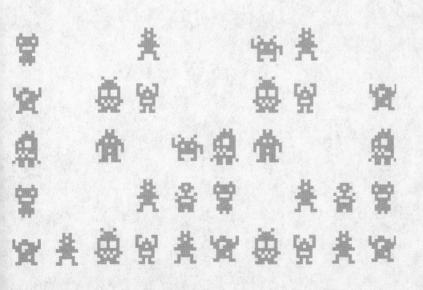

CHAPTER
THREE

My mom had only been married to Neil for three weeks the first time I got a clear picture of him.

It was a Wednesday night, which used to just mean my mom would make rigatoni and meatballs and we'd sit on the couch to watch *Family Feud*. Since the wedding, though, Neil was always wanting to do things together. School had just let out for the year, and he decided that we were all going out to eat at Captain Spaulding's. As a family.

The restaurant was the loud, sticky kind where people go to sit around a table for an hour, eating onion rings and acting like they're having a good time.

Billy didn't even bother to pretend. He spent the whole meal leaning back in his chair and staring at the ceiling.

My mom picked at her salad for a while, then reached over and put her hand on mine. "You know, I was thinking that maybe this summer, we could sign you up for volleyball camp?"

"It's not really we, since you don't have to go."

My mom smiled a big, anxious smile, and I saw there was lipstick on her teeth. "It would be a good way to spend time with other girls for a change. Don't you want to make some new friends?" The waxy smear made her look like she'd been eating something bloody. I frowned and stopped looking at it.

Neil was eating his cheeseburger with a fork and knife. He stopped chewing and leaned close, staring into my face. "You answer your mother."

I twisted away. "Why? It doesn't matter what I want." His breath smelled like pickles.

"Maxine," he said. "I'm warning you."

"My name," I said, feeling a hot rush of fury in my cheeks, "is *Max*."

Neil breathed through his nose like he was trying to keep something locked inside. Then he set down his fork and reached for my arm. "If you don't get that mouth under control, you're going to be one sorry little girl."

And I knew I was supposed to apologize and act like the good, smiling daughter my mom and Neil wanted me to be, but I could feel everything inside me speeding up. It was like being stuck in class for the whole afternoon, and then the bell rings and all you want is to get outside and go and go and go. My dad always said that my brain was fast but my mouth was faster.

"I'd rather be sorry than be at volleyball camp."

Neil gave me a level stare that seemed to burrow its way under my skin. "You need to learn a thing or two about how you talk to your father."

"But you're not my father." I said it very quietly, just under my breath.

Not quietly enough.

Neil tightened his grip on my arm and pulled me out of my chair. "You're done here. Go wait in the car."

I stared at my plate, still heaped with fruit salad and french fries and the rest of my hamburger. We were supposed to get sundaes after. "I haven't even finished my fries!"

Neil gave me a long, freezing stare, like something inside him was turning to ice while I watched. "Wait. In the car."

I stared back until the weight of his gaze got too heavy to stand, and then I looked away.

I wasn't going to cry. I told myself he was just another temporary interruption to my life—I just had to wait him out. But I didn't really believe it. Things were changing too fast. My mom had never sent me away from the table. I wasn't crying. But almost.

I walked stiffly out of the restaurant, past the waitresses

and the hostess. I was mortified by the way they looked at me, like they knew I was in trouble and were sorry for me. I was almost thirteen and the whole restaurant was watching me get time-out like a little kid.

Out in the parking lot, I sat in the backseat of my mom's Skylark with the door open and thought about how much I hated Neil.

I'd found half a package of sunflower seeds in the pocket of my shorts and was eating them and dropping the shells on the ground when I realized that someone was standing over me.

Billy had come outside and was standing in the pale yellow circle of the streetlight, looking down at me.

After a long time, he sighed and lit a cigarette. He always smoked them in this insolent punk-rock way, clamping the butt between his teeth so it jutted from the center of his mouth. "You really did it this time, declaring war on Neil."

I didn't want him to see how stupid I felt for yelling at his dad and getting sent away from the table. I scowled and looked down at my shoes. They were green suede Vans. The color on the toes was scuffing, but the rubber was all right. "I just don't want him acting like he's my dad, and I'm not going to pretend that he is."

"Don't worry about it," Billy said, looking up at the neon CAPTAIN SPAULDING's sign. The waving, smiling clown flashed over the parking lot. "It's not like he's my dad either."

I glanced at him, not sure I'd heard right. "What?"

Billy turned back to me, and I was sure he was going to tell me it would be okay. Maybe even hug me.

But his eyes were flat and heavy like always. "He's a horrible guy, Max. Haven't you figured that out? You really think a guy like that could be a father? Not to me, and not to you."

• • •

"You don't want to wear your costume?" my mom said when I came into the kitchen for breakfast on my second day of school. She was unwrapping dishes from a cardboard box full of newspapers and putting them in the cupboard.

Neil was at the table, eating scrambled eggs and reading the sports page. He shoved the last bite of toast into his mouth and answered her, even though she'd been talking to me. "You shouldn't encourage her. She's getting too old for that."

My mom gave me a shy, apologetic look, but she didn't argue with him. I just rolled my eyes and reached past her for the cereal. *Whatever.*

Anyway, it felt wrong to get ready for Halloween alone. Usually, I spent all of October hanging out in the garage with Nate, working on our costumes and thinking up cool ways to beg for candy when people came to their doors, and now I was two thousand miles away and it felt like an entire chunk of myself was missing.

I'd been a little bit of a fanatic about Halloween ever

since I was tiny. It was the perfect holiday. Maybe not my favorite—Christmas was still pretty rad, even though it was cheesy to admit that—but Halloween was the one night I got to feel like something bigger than just myself.

The year before, I'd gone as Nosferatu, and Nate was Dr. Van Helsing. He colored his hair gray with baby powder and had a canvas bag of wooden tent stakes, but no one could tell who he was supposed to be, even when he took out one of the stakes and pretended to stab me. His turned out pretty good, but my costume was scarier, with jagged plastic teeth and a rubber cap to make me look bald. My mom was practically distraught over how ugly it was, when that was the whole point.

Ever since I was little, I had loved monsters. I never missed an episode of *Darkroom,* and sometimes my dad would take me to the Bluebird Theater, where they showed old black-and-white movies full of mummies and wolfmen and Frankensteins.

Lately, though, I was more into movie slashers like Leatherface and Jason, or the guy in this new one they kept showing previews for, who had a ratty striped sweater and a face like Sloppy Joes. There were all kinds of monsters with superpowers and magical abilities, but slashers seemed scarier because they were less imaginary. Sure, a vampire was creepy, but psycho killers could actually happen. I mean, I saw the news. Creepy guys in dark alleys or white vans went after girls all the time.

After breakfast, I stood in the hall to my bedroom, trying to decide what to do. I hadn't really planned to wear the costume, but the way Neil had written it off without even looking at me and the way he'd talked to my mom made me want to, just to piss him off. I was pretty sure I knew where my mask was.

The moving boxes were all still piled in the corner of my bedroom, labeled with my mom's neat, fussy writing. When I opened the one marked *Max's Treasures,* the mask was there, lying on top of my Flash comics like a floppy rubber nightmare.

I'd picked Michael Myers from *Halloween* because he had no weaknesses. He never moved fast, but he still caught up to you every time. He was impossibly strong—you couldn't overpower him and you couldn't outrun him. He was unstoppable.

Nate had been planning to go as Shaggy from *Scooby-Doo* because his mom never let him see R-rated movies. Mine probably wouldn't either, but I didn't have to worry about that because there was always my dad. *Had* always been my dad.

Michael Myers was the kind of monster I was most afraid of, because he was real. Not real-life, but the kind you could believe in anyway. He never talked or took his mask off, but underneath he was still a man, and a man could be lurking anywhere. There are all kinds of dangerous things in the world. Maybe not exactly like him, but close enough. You can't avoid them, so sometimes you just have to learn how to live with them.

The mask was white rubber, with molded plastic eyebrows and a wig of thick black hair and blank everything else, and I stood looking down at it, trying to decide whether I was going to put it on.

"Ma-aaax," Billy called from out in the hall. I knew he was in a mood when he called to me in that singsong voice that sounded sweet on top and dangerous underneath. "Where the hell are you, Max?"

I threw the mask on the bed and started digging through the box for the rest of the costume—maybe not the coverall, but the machete at least. I picked up a House of Mystery anthology and dropped it on the floor, trying to find the machete, but it was buried somewhere at the bottom, and I was running out of time.

From out in the hall, Billy called to me again. His voice had changed. He was farther away now. "If you're not in the car in ten seconds, I'm leaving without you."

I hurried out to the living room, still holding my mask. He raised his eyebrows when he saw it, but didn't say anything.

I shrugged and gave the mask a shake. "It's Halloween."

He still didn't answer, just looked at me with bored, heavy eyes.

"What? Now I'm not even allowed to dress up?"

"Go ahead, but don't be shocked when you look like a

baby. No one in middle school dresses up for Halloween. It's for losers, okay?"

I shrugged, but it was small and empty. When I couldn't think of anything to say, I went back into my room and shoved the mask in my dresser. One more thing that had stopped being mine.

CHAPTER FOUR

Even though I'd caved to Billy about the costume, I'd still sort of thought I was going to show up to Hawkins Middle in my everyday clothes and find a sea of mummies and witches. But no one else was dressed up either. As much as I didn't want to admit it, I was a little grateful not to be the new girl and the only person wearing a costume.

I was getting used to the school, but compared with the one I'd gone to at home, it seemed sprawled out and plain. The way there were no skylights and no windows made it feel like everything had stalled and I was stuck in an alternate reality that was all fluorescent lights and linoleum. I needed to move.

When the slow, sticky feeling finally got so bad I couldn't take it anymore, I dropped my board and rode it lazily through the halls. I was pretty sure that wasn't actually allowed, but I needed to do something that made the floor stop feeling like quicksand.

I was at my locker, trading out my books, when someone cleared their throat behind me. When I turned around, two of the stalker boys who'd been watching me out by the football field yesterday at lunch were standing side by side. One had thick, curly hair that stood out around his head and a broad, sunny face. He was beaming like he'd never had a better day. The other was a wiry black kid with a short 'fro. His smile was steadier and less intense but nice.

They were dressed like Ray Stantz and Peter Venkman from *Ghostbusters*. When they'd showed up to science that morning, everyone had giggled and whispered, but the costumes were pretty good. I thought about the mask in my dresser. Even if my mom had told me I couldn't wear it and made me go as something else, I wouldn't have picked *Ghostbusters*. It was a good movie, but the whole point of Halloween was to be something scary.

The curly-headed one was talking before I could even work out what they were doing there. "Hi, Max, I'm Dustin, and this is—"

The other one was less frenetic. I'd noticed him yesterday, because he was watching me from behind a fence. But also because there were basically no black kids in Hawkins. "Lucas," he said.

The look I gave them was bored and scornful. "Yeah, I know. The stalkers."

They both started talking at once, bumbling over themselves. Dustin launched into a hectic monologue. I couldn't tell if he was just nervous or if he was trying to sell me on something. He sounded like he was pulling some kind of scam, like the scalpers who were always trying to get you to buy concert tickets outside the clubs in LA.

He and Lucas were rambling over each other, and it took me a minute to figure out what they were even saying. Finally, Dustin looked at me wide-eyed, like he'd just had a revelation. "You're new here, so you probably don't have any friends to take you trick-or-treating."

It was rude to say it, maybe, but he was obviously right.

He grinned, showing white, even front teeth. "We're all meeting at the Maple Street cul-de-sac. Seven on the dot."

I'd come to Hawkins with no plans to fit in or be popular or make friends or anything, but it was hard to remember that now. They were smiling, and I stared back, trying to understand whether this was all some kind of game. Whether they really wanted me to come with them. I'd spent so much time hanging around Billy it was getting harder and harder to tell when something was serious and when it was a joke.

. . .

I'd always thought I was good at being on my own. Independent, not afraid to take the bus downtown by myself or climb under the fence at the impound lot just to see what was in there.

But I'd never actually spent a lot of time without my friends. We were always doing projects together, or else making plans to. After school and in the summer, we spent pretty much every day building forts or skating in the park.

Nate Walker had been my very best friend since we were six. He was shorter and skinnier than me, with knobby elbows and the kind of mouse-brown hair that no one stared at or made fiery-redhead jokes about. We were field-trip buddies and science partners and we played street hockey and camped out in my backyard and it didn't even matter that I was a girl.

On the first day of first grade, I saw this skinny little boy in a red Spider-Man shirt crouched under the slide at lunch. Some of the other boys had been chasing him with a dead worm on a stick until he started crying and then ran away to hide. Even at six, I thought it seemed like a pretty pointless thing to cry over, but I liked his shirt, so I crawled under and sat with him.

"What's wrong?" I said. The air under the slide was hot. I can still remember the way the sand made my hands feel like chalk.

He ducked his head and didn't answer.

"Do you want to see my Man-Thing comic?" I said, and he nodded and wiped his nose on his arm.

The Man-Thing comic was a million years old, and the cover was falling off because I liked to take it everywhere. In it, the Man-Thing has to battle an evil biker gang that's been hanging around his swamp, along with a shady developer who wants to destroy him. The developer hires a corrupt scientist to invent a trap called the Slaughter Room in order to get rid of him, but the Man-Thing escapes and kills the leader of the biker gang before shambling back into the swamp.

We sat with our shoulders pressed together and read the book right up until the yard monitor came over to lean under the slide and say that it was time to go back in.

After that, we were friends. I always picked him first for dodgeball, even though he was so bad at blocking and someone always tagged him out right away. He always knew how to fix his bike or my skateboard and didn't care too much when I got competitive about H-O-R-S-E or sounded like I was mad about something when I was really just asking a question.

My dad still lived with us then, and most of the time, he didn't have much of an opinion about my friends one way or the other, but he liked Nate. Ben was too hyper, and to my dad, Eddie might as well have been a cinder block or a potato, but Nate, he would always say, was one to watch. Bright.

My dad didn't care much about good grades, or whether

someone had the right clothes or car, or came from the right neighborhood, but he liked when people were bright.

And Nate was. He was shyer and softer than the other guys we hung out with, but he was smart and interesting and always had the best ideas for how to build a tree fort or make a catapult work. Anyway, it was nice, sometimes, to hang out with someone who didn't always need to be moving as fast as I did.

Nate actually understood what my dad meant when he talked about hailstorms or carburetors, and I liked that. He never acted like it was weird that while other people's parents listened to Neil Diamond or the Bee Gees, my dad listened to bands that came on bootleg cassette tapes with strips of masking tape on them with the names written in marker. The music was angry and screamy, and the bands were called things like the Dead Kennedys and Agent Orange and the Bags. My mom just sighed, got out the vacuum cleaner or the mixer, and pretended she didn't hear.

I didn't like the bootleg tapes as much as my dad did. I was more into the Go-Go's, and sometimes old surfer music like the Beach Boys, or else the Sandals, who did the soundtrack to *The Endless Summer,* but when my dad put on one of his punk bands, Nate lit up like he was hearing something I wasn't. I didn't get what was so great about the music, but it felt good to bring my friends home to someone who liked them. The memory of my dad was hazy and warm.

Now I just had Billy and Neil and no place to feel good about and no one to bring home anyway.

• • •

By the time school let out, I was about ready to climb out of my skin. The day already felt a million years long.

I packed up my books, then skated along the cracked blacktop back up to the high school parking lot. Back to the Camaro.

Billy was waiting, leaning on the back bumper and smoking a cigarette. He was looking away from me, toward the pale autumn sky, and I waited to find out which version of him I'd get today.

You never knew with Billy. That was sort of the worst thing about him—how sometimes he wasn't that bad. Especially at first, before I'd figured out what he was like, I actually enjoyed hanging out with him. He picked me up from school sometimes, or let me go with him to Kragen Auto. The problem was, he could be fun.

He didn't treat me the way he treated the girls he went to school with, maybe just because they were older or less willing to stick up for themselves, but I thought it might be something else.

When he took them to parties or to hang out in the Carl's Jr. parking lot with the other wasters from school, it wasn't like a date. And sure, they acted like they were too cool to care about going steady or being someone's girl-friend, but they still tried to get him to come over and meet their parents, or made a big thing of being nice to me, like that was somehow going to impress him. They held their breath, hoping it would mean something, and then a week later, he'd be pulling into the Carl's Jr. with someone else.

It was like he hated them, except he still took them up to Sunset Cliffs to make out. It infuriated me, the way boys acted like girls couldn't be interesting or human and were only good for taking off their shirts.

Billy never treated me that way, though. At first I thought it was because I was younger or because I was his sister, even if I wasn't his real one. But after a while, I started to understand that the reason he treated me differently was because I wasn't like them. I didn't chase boys or wear makeup or even always remember to brush my hair. And for most of my life, the reason had been simple: I hadn't wanted to. But now the rules were different, and it felt more like I couldn't.

Billy talked to me, but in this sly, confidential way, like there was something important he wanted me to understand. It was like he hated me, except for the way he went out of his way to make me just like him. Any hint of softness and he would never let me forget it.

On the ride home, I slouched in the passenger seat, listening to him go on about what a backwater Hawkins was—the hick party scene, the speed limits, the terrible basketball team, the lame girls.

I was staring out the window, watching the countryside flash by—woods and fields. There were so many trees. I knew he wanted me to agree with him and say how much the place sucked, but I didn't see the point, and I told him that—how we were stuck here, so we might as well deal with it.

He turned on me. "And whose fault is that?"

For a second I was sure this was finally it—we were going to talk about what had happened back in San Diego. I didn't want to, and maybe if I kept quiet, we wouldn't have to deal with it.

But Billy had gone brutal and chilly, waiting for me to take the blame. "Say it."

When I didn't answer, he turned in his seat and screamed it at me, his voice a raw, ugly roar. "Say it!"

He gunned the engine and we charged along the two-lane road, scattering drifts of orange leaves. I stared straight ahead and didn't say anything.

In front of us, the road wound lazily through the wooded countryside. We came over the top of a little hill to see a straggly line of bikes. Three boys in brown coveralls with oversize proton packs on their backs. Ghostbusters. They were pedaling down the road, spread out across the right-hand lane.

"Billy, slow down."

"Oh, are these your new hick friends?" Billy mashed his foot down harder. "I get bonus points if I get 'em all in one go?"

The needle on the speedometer was climbing. Ahead of us, the Ghostbusters were still cruising down the middle of the road. They couldn't see us.

"Billy, come on, stop! It's not funny!"

He turned in the driver's seat, looking at me instead of the road. The stereo was blasting and he bobbed his head, thrashing along to the music.

The boys were an interruption in the road, getting bigger. We were coming up on them at an impossible speed, and they finally looked around. I could see their confusion, and I felt the same thing on my own face, because it couldn't mean what it seemed to. Billy wasn't going to run them down, that would be insane. It was the kind of thing people joked about but didn't actually *do*.

I told myself that, but there was no way for me to believe it. In a normal, orderly world, this couldn't happen. But the truth was here, right in front of me: I didn't know what Billy was going to do about anything anymore.

The bikes loomed in front of us. They looked totally destructible.

I knew if I didn't do something, everything after this moment was going to be bad. The fear was in my throat now, a clawing, squeezing hand. I reached across the center console and shoved the wheel. The Camaro swerved out into the oncoming lane.

There was a wild jolt, like everything was sliding. Tires squealed. Then we were around the boys and bombing down the road toward home.

I looked back over my shoulder, in time to see them all lying on the shoulder, bikes tipped sideways in the drifts of leaves.

The danger was behind us now, but my eyes felt hot and too big for my head. It was hard for me to blink, and I stared at the dirty windshield. At the road.

As soon as my hand had touched the steering wheel, I'd known that I was doing something dangerous. I'd crossed some invisible dividing line into a place where bad things happened, and now I would have to pay for it. Billy would scream at me, kick me out of the car and make me walk. Maybe even hurt me.

He didn't even seem to care, though. He just threw his head back and laughed a high, screaming laugh, huge and hilarious, like this was all some messed-up game. "That was a close one!"

He was grinning, drumming on the steering wheel and nodding along to the music. I kept my hand on the door handle all the way home.

I was thinking about something my dad had told me. The trick to being at home in the world, he said, was knowing how to do things. If you had the right tools, you could fix your own sink, find a job, figure out a problem. It was why he cared so much about knowledge and information. It was why I tried so hard to learn the things he taught me.

When you can take apart a hinge or pick a lock, you can always get out.

CHAPTER FIVE

As soon as we pulled up to the house, I got out and went inside.

My heart was beating like a piston in my chest. I needed to distract myself. I went straight to my bedroom and started digging through my boxes, looking for the rest of my costume. It was down in the bottom of the moving box, wadded up under a stack of surf magazines.

Some of the girls in my history class had been talking about trick-or-treating and where to get the best haul. It had made me feel better, a little, to find out that even if it was suddenly deeply uncool to go to class dressed up, the kids in Hawkins still went out on Halloween.

The main part of the costume was an old coverall of my dad's from when he had a very temporary job as a washing-machine repairman. It had been too big for me, and the zipper stuck. I'd been working on my costume since the second week in September, and my mom wasn't a huge fan of the idea that I wanted to be Michael Myers, but she'd still dragged out her sewing machine and cut the coverall down to fit me. That was as far as she'd been willing to go, though. She said I couldn't have a machete, but my dad had come to the rescue. He found a giant deli knife at a swap meet in LA and ground down the blade to look more like the one in the movie.

It was a good costume, and suddenly I didn't care about the kids at school or Billy or whether Neil said I was too old. I was going trick-or-treating.

I pawed through the box and laid the knife and the coverall on the bed next to my mask. It hit me all at once that this was the first time I'd be spending Halloween without my best friends. Then I closed my eyes and reminded myself that even if we'd stayed in San Diego, it wouldn't have been the same. Even before we moved, things had changed.

At least the *Ghostbuster* boys had invited me to trick-or-treat with them. That wasn't so bad. I had a costume and someplace to go.

I put on my coverall and my mask and let myself won-der what kind of candy they gave out here. It was better than thinking about the drive home. I didn't want to picture what would have happened if I hadn't grabbed the wheel. It was over. They were fine.

But my hands felt shaky.

• • •

The thing about Billy was you never knew what was going to happen when he got mad.

The week after school let out for the summer in San Diego, he'd gotten in trouble for trespassing, and Neil had grounded him. There was a construction site across the street from the high school—some kind of apartments or offices—and Billy and his friends liked to hang out there, drinking beers and sitting around on the scaffolding. Then someone from the construction crew must have noticed the empty cans or the cigarette butts everywhere and called the cops.

We were at home in the living room one Saturday night. I'd been supposed to go visit my dad, but at the last minute, Neil had changed his mind and said that I'd been seeing too much of him lately, and I should spend more weekends with my mom. So I stayed in San Diego and baked cookies with my mom and carved *I hate Neil* into the baseboard behind the couch in tiny letters using a safety pin.

I was sitting on the floor watching the NBC weekly movie and eating Count Chocula in my pajamas when the cops brought Billy home. He was dirty and rumpled, with mud on his boots and a cut on his hand, but mostly he just looked furious. The cops said that he and his friends had been up in the scaffolding at the construction site, daring each other to walk across the steel I beams.

I wasn't always good at being careful with people or at making small talk, but I was good at guessing their moods. Even when I was little, I could sometimes tell just by looking who was dangerous or who was lying. My mom would stare at me wonderingly, and once, when I told her the guy she was dating had a gambling problem, she asked how anyone could know that. In that case, it wasn't like I was doing some impossible trick. His pockets were full of lottery tickets and betting stubs. The only reason I knew and she didn't was because she never believed the signs until it was too late.

I hadn't ever told her about Billy, but I should have. I just hadn't gotten to it yet. I kept waiting for her to see without me having to say it. The again, maybe it wouldn't have made a difference.

Neil waited until the cops were gone, then turned with a face like thunder. He told Billy that he could either sign up for junior ROTC, or say goodbye to his car for the next two months. Billy said goodbye to the car.

A week later, I was up on the weedy little ridge behind the house. A creek bed ran along the top of the hill. In the spring, it filled with four and a half feet of dirty, fast-moving water, but now it was dry and would be for the rest of the year.

I'd spent most of my summers hanging out up there with

Nate and Ben and Eddie. We had a little spot, with packed dirt and a table made out of a wooden milk crate, and a mangy couch that Ben and Eddie had found set out by the curb on trash day. It wasn't a clubhouse, exactly, but we'd go up there to shoot BB guns at bottles, or else get Bomb Pops from the Good Humor truck and hang out on the couch, talking about monster trucks or wrestling and sucking on the Popsicles until our teeth turned blue.

Usually Nate would come over at nine or ten. We'd spend the morning reading comics, then take his bike and my skateboard to the park, or else ride over to the pool with Ben and Eddie. But Eddie was in Sacramento for the weekend, and Ben had to mow his parents' yard. Nate was visiting his dad, so I was alone.

I'd been working on our latest project, which was a real working catapult. When it was done, we were going to use it to chuck water balloons at the road. I'd spent the morning getting the firing arm to swing, but now it was afternoon and hot, and I was just sitting on the back of the couch with my shoes on the cushions, looking out over the road that ran along the bottom of the hill.

Billy was inside, hanging around with his friends. Neil had taken his keys, and now the Camaro sat in the garage like a dog in a kennel, waiting for its owner to come let it out. He was supposed to be painting the garage, but he only worked on it when his dad was around.

Wayne and Sid were both from the housing development on the other side of the ridge. They went to school with

Billy and looked scraggly and dangerous, but I got the idea that they mostly just followed him around and let him tell them what to do.

I liked Sid the best. He was tall and sort of pudgy, with big, heavy-knuckled hands and green laces in his combat boots. He was usually nice and could be kind of funny, but he didn't talk very much.

Wayne was louder and skinnier, with greasy hair down to his shoulders and a face like a weasel. Since Neil had taken the keys to the Camaro, they mostly hung out in Billy's room, listening to Metallica and Ratt, but it must have been getting old, because that day Billy brought them out to the hill behind the house.

I wasn't sure I wanted them lounging around in my private hideout. I'd already had to learn how to exist in the same house as Billy, and now he was invading the rest of my life too. Since the night the cops brought him home, he'd been in a rank mood, slamming through the house or locking himself in his room and playing his music as loud as it would go, but that day, the three of them came crunching out to the creek bed and sat down next to me on the couch.

Billy leaned back and lit a cigarette, then stared off at the sprawling neighborhood below. For a while, we all sat and watched the traffic at the bottom of the hill without saying anything.

Sid had a Music City catalog and was leafing through it

looking at guitars. Wayne was jumpy and restless. He kept getting up to pace around in the weeds above the creek, then sitting back down again.

Finally, he threw his arms out and spun in a circle. "This sucks, man. I can't believe your dad jacked your car."

Billy was sitting on the edge of the couch, his eyes fixed on the road. The day had seemed heavy and lazy before, but now he looked tense, like he was waiting for something to happen. He gave Wayne a bored stare, then blew out a long plume of smoke and took out his lighter. It was a silver-colored flip-top with a flaming-skull decal, and I'd always been a little envious of it. Now, though, Billy was staring too hard at the weeds and dry scrub brush that grew all over the hill. The lighter flashed in the sunlight. I didn't like looking at it.

There was a dead cat that had been lying under one of the sweet pea bushes for a while. A mangy orange tom with one white foot. I didn't recognize it from the neighborhood, so it had probably been a stray, but I still felt sorry for it. I figured it must have gotten hit by a car and then crawled up the hill to die.

I'd been interested in it at first, but now I hated to look at it. The way the swarms of flies and beetles crawled over its fur gave me a squirmy feeling. I hated how its sides got flatter and more matted every day.

"Nasty!" said Wayne. He was leaning down with his hands braced on his knees, squinting into the bushes. "Look at this thing. Its ear's all messed up. I bet it used to be a total brawler. Do you think if I got some pliers, we could pull out its teeth for a necklace?"

"Gross, no!" I said, watching from my spot on the back of the couch.

Billy gave me a bored look and then got up and sauntered over to Wayne. The sun looked silver, glinting off his earring. His expression didn't change. "Or we could pay our respects and give it a Viking funeral. What do you think, *Sid*?"

He said it in a hard, bright voice, and I saw that something was ugly between them, but I couldn't tell what.

Sid didn't answer. I was sitting above him on the back of the couch, and he turned to me, holding up the catalog and pointing at an ad for a sleek cream-colored guitar. "This one's a Kramer Baretta. It's got a slanted humbucker, just like the Frankenstrat that Eddie Van Halen plays on 'Hot for Teacher.' See this little plate under the strings?"

I nodded and stared dutifully at the picture, even though I didn't know the first thing about guitars or what a humbucker was.

Over by the body of the cat, Wayne was laughing. "You're the one who said it would be cool to see one. At least Billy's got the balls to be a man about it!"

Sid slouched next to me, staring at the catalog. He folded the corner on the Kramer Baretta and didn't look up. "You mean, do the dumbest thing possible?"

I looked at them, but I couldn't figure out what it was or what was happening. "What's a Viking funeral?"

Billy grinned and rolled his head in my direction. "You really want to know?" He flicked the lighter and held it up, looking at me through the flame. "Ask Sid."

Sid still didn't look up from the catalog, just shook his head. "Seriously, cut it out."

I was hoping he'd explain, but Wayne was the one who answered, popping his eyes wide. "They used to light their dead on fire. Sid knows all about it. He got a hundred on the final history paper. Didn't you, Sid?"

I knew the paper. Billy had gotten a D, and Neil had been irate. Sid didn't say anything.

The cat was mostly decomposed and very dead, but it had still been an actual living, breathing animal. "No," I said. "That's gross. Don't."

It had been lying under the sweet pea for almost two weeks and was starting to get pretty mummified. It would have been dry enough on its own, probably, but Billy wasn't taking chances. He reached into his pocket and took out the little can of butane that he used to refill his lighter.

Without looking away from me, he popped the cap and sprayed the butane over the cat.

I watched as the lighter fluid splashed over the sunken shape of its body.

He and Wayne both leaned down for a closer look. Then Billy held the lighter under the bush. I wanted to jump up and knock the lighter out of his hand. I wanted to scream for him to stop, but it wouldn't have made a difference.

There was a long silence, like we were all holding our breath, and then he flicked the wheel with his thumb.

When the fur caught, it went in a dry, rasping whoosh. Wayne stumbled back, whooping and slapping at the bottom of his vest. The leaping flames had singed the tail of his shirt. Billy watched him with the strangest look—almost like he was satisfied.

The smell of the burning cat was like garbage and scorched hair, and I covered my nose with my hand. I watched it burn and reminded myself that nothing could hurt it now. The cat had probably had a rough life, but this new assault was nothing to it. It was already dead.

The weeds around the ditch were dry and yellow, even though it was only June, and the grass around the cat caught fire almost at once. I watched as the fire raced in a low stripe along the edge of the ditch. It looked almost liquid, spilling through the grass.

"What the hell, man?" Wayne was still cursing and slapping at his shirt. But he was laughing that high, giddy laugh, yelping and clutching his hand.

The fire was the color of a melted Creamsicle. It rushed out from the body of the cat and began to lick its way down the slope of the hill toward the road.

Sid threw down his guitar magazine and jumped up. He crossed the clearing in three lumbering steps and began to stomp hard on the burning grass with his army boots. I watched for a second, then climbed down from the couch and ran after him, stepping on the places he'd missed, kicking dirt over the embers.

It was a little while before we got it under control. Wayne was still skipping and wriggling like a puppy, laughing his high, manic giggle. Billy just watched, standing over the burning cat, smiling that small, tight smile he got when something seemed funny to him.

Finally, everything was extinguished, and Sid trudged back up the hill, breathing hard. The fire was out, but there was a blackened strip of grass for twelve feet along the edge of the ditch. Later I sat on my bed and counted all the places where the soles of my shoes had melted.

All summer, whenever I went up behind the house to the creek and saw that burned place, I would remember the way Billy had looked right before he flicked the lighter. I would smell the dead, burning stink again. A smoky, spoiled smell that sat in my nose like a warning. The cat wasn't a cat at all anymore, just a greasy black spot on the ground. The bush where it had been was mostly burned away, just blackened twigs and ashes.

After that, I knew.

Not that Billy was crazy or out of control, exactly—it wasn't like the cat had been alive. But the fact that he'd done it meant *some*thing.

I was getting good at staying out of his way when he got

mad, but I never seemed to be able to predict it ahead of time. I could never be sure what he was going to do.

• • •

At the corner of Oak and Maple, Billy pulled up to the curb and let me out. My mom had said he was supposed to come with me and walk me around the neighborhood, but both of us knew that wasn't going to happen. He was dressed for some high school party, in a leather jacket and fingerless gloves. It wasn't much of a costume, but I didn't say so.

"You be waiting here at ten," he told me, leaning out the driver's-side window. "If you're not here when I get back, too bad."

I nodded and pulled my mask down over my face.

He flicked a cigarette butt out the window and gunned the engine, already looking off toward something I couldn't see. I stood and watched the taillights go blazing away down the street. They turned the corner and were gone.

The neighborhood was crowded with trick-or-treaters, and I rubbed my arms through the coverall. I still wasn't used to how cold it got at night. Little kids raced back and forth across the road, running from one house to the next, their bags and buckets and pillowcases flapping. The air was crisp and chilly, but no one was wearing jackets.

I stood at the end of the Maple Street cul-de-sac, waiting for the Ghostbusters. I was a little worried that they might not want to see me after what Billy had done, but I'd decided to chance it. Anything was better than sitting alone in my room with no place to go and nothing to do. They'd invited me. And anyway, it hadn't been like I was the one who tried to run them down.

I'd just been the one who'd been right there watching from the passenger seat. Great. Maybe they'd blame me and not show up at all.

But I'd only been waiting a few minutes when, down the street, I saw the familiar shapes of boys in proton packs. There were four of them—Lucas and Dustin, along with the other two who'd been watching me from behind the fence during lunch yesterday. They were all in my science class and sat together in a little block of desks up near the front.

They looked so happy and oblivious, just bopping along, not paying attention to anything around them, and suddenly I had an idea to jump out at them. I wanted to shake things up, not enough to really scare anyone, but enough to make a little bit of a scene.

When I leapt out of the shadows with my machete, it was even better than I'd pictured. They all jumped and screamed high, shuddery screams, and I laughed—really laughed—for the first time since we'd moved to Hawkins. Lucas screamed the loudest. Normally that would have given me a mean, antsy feeling, like I needed to rag on him a little, but in a weird way it was kind of cute.

We headed for the Loch Nora subdivision, which was just off Main Street. At home, that would have meant a bunch of dive bars and walk-up apartments. But even though it was so close to downtown, it was the nicest neighborhood in Hawkins. The street was wide, lined with big two-story houses that all had picture windows and lawns planted with election signs.

My mom didn't usually care much about voting, but this year she'd paid more attention to the election. Before she and Neil were married, she used to talk about Walter Mondale sometimes. Mostly she would just shake her head and say how crazy he was to pick that Ferraro woman to be his vice president, because no man wanted to vote for a woman, even a woman with a law degree. But I thought it was kind of cool. Once, after the wedding, I tried to ask her who she thought she'd vote for, but Neil told me to knock off that political talk at the dinner table. Then he said how Reagan was the best thing that had happened to this country since Eisenhower, and there was no way in hell that anyone in his house was voting for Mondale and that lady. Most of the yard signs in Loch Nora were for Reagan.

We raced through the neighborhood, knocking on doors and holding out our bags for Snickers and Kit Kats. The other two boys were named Will and Mike, and neither of them really looked at me or said much. Mike had thick, dark hair and a pale, serious face. Will was smaller and quieter than the others and reminded me a little of my friend Nate. He seemed like the kind of boy people didn't usually notice.

For some reason, he was hauling around a huge camcorder almost too big for him to carry. He seemed shy and easy to embarrass, like the kind of person who probably felt weird having his picture taken. I wondered if it was easier when he could be the one looking out from behind the lens.

As we ran from house to house, I had to admit I was glad they'd invited me. They were awkward and hyper and a little dorky, but they were being really nice to me.

All except Mike. He sulked along behind us with a sour expression, and every time I glanced back at him, he would look away like he hoped I would just disappear.

The way he kept ignoring me was obnoxious, but there was no point in picking a fight with him. We were supposed to be having fun. So I made a point to have the most fun I could have. Walking between Lucas and Dustin, the night felt warmer, and I could almost forget that I was a million miles away from my friends and my dad and my entire life.

Loch Nora was clean and a lot fancier than anyplace I'd lived back home. By the time we'd cruised both sides of the street, my bag was so heavy that the bottom sagged, full of mini boxes of Nerds and full-size Milky Ways. The town might be the size of a postage stamp, but the candy was top-shelf.

We were standing on the edge of someone's lawn, comparing our hauls, when we looked around and noticed that Will was gone.

The street stretched dark and empty in both directions, and I had no idea how we were supposed to find him, but

Mike was already off and running, darting around the side of one of the big brick houses.

The backyard was lower than the front, and you got to it by going down a little set of stairs next to the house. Mike plunged down them, and we followed.

Will was there at the bottom, sitting in the shadows. The way he was curled in on himself made it hard to see him at first. He looked crumpled and strange, like he was frozen in place.

Mike was crouched in front of him, holding him by the shoulders. "I'm gonna get you home." When Lucas and Dustin crowded closer and tried to help them up, though, Mike shrugged them off and put his arm around Will. "Keep trick-or-treating. I'm bored anyway."

He might have been worried, but he sounded angry. He was talking to all of us, but I had a feeling it was because of me—because I was staring too intently or too long, or maybe just because I was there at all.

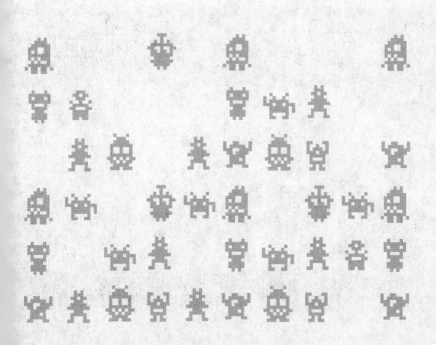

CHAPTER SIX

I walked into the house just past eleven o'clock, with my mask pushed up onto my forehead and my bag of candy slung over my shoulder. My feet hurt all the way up to my knees, and my hands were so cold that I could hardly feel them. So much for the unseasonably warm night. I'd spent almost half an hour waiting for Billy on the corner of Oak Street, but after the porch lights started flicking off and the last trick-or-treaters disappeared into their houses, I knew what I should have known from the start: he wasn't coming.

As soon as I got home, my mom came drifting out into the living room in her nightgown with cold cream on her face. "What in the world were you doing out so late? Where's your brother?"

Neil sat up straighter in his armchair. "I'd be interested to know the same thing."

For a second, I just stood in the middle of the living room, trying to figure out how to answer. I had a sudden urge to tell them that Billy wasn't my brother, even though that seemed like the least important part of the whole equation.

I shrugged and looked away. "Nowhere. There was this guy he knows from school who needed a ride home, so Billy dropped me off first. He'll be back in a second."

The lie was so ridiculous it made my face hot, but it still seemed better to avoid the truth, if I wanted to keep Neil from going ballistic. If I ever wanted to be allowed out of the house again.

My mom was watching me doubtfully, but she nodded. Her eyes were so hopeful, and I could see that she wanted to believe me. It was the same way people like her always got duped. It never mattered what the lie was; they just wanted so badly to believe it.

We were still standing in the living room, facing each other, when the quiet outside was interrupted by the sound of the Camaro. We all turned toward the door.

When Billy came slamming into the house, the smell came with him, rolling like the clouds of smoke and alcohol wafting out of a dive bar. Like bad weather. He was stumbling a little. His eyes were red-rimmed and heavier than ever, and he still had the leather jacket on, but he wasn't wearing a shirt. The light from the stained-glass lamp on the end table made him look deranged.

Neil breathed in through his nose and heaved himself out of his chair. "And where the hell have you been?"

"Nowhere," Billy muttered, and tried to brush past him, but Neil stepped in front of him and stopped him with a hand on his chest.

"What was that?"

Billy ducked his head and mumbled something about a flat tire. I couldn't tell if he was being honest or not—probably not—but as soon as he said it, it was pretty obvious that I had been lying. Whatever he'd been doing, it definitely hadn't been giving a school friend a ride home.

My mom gasped and turned on me with big, hurt eyes. "Why didn't you tell us he *left* you?"

She sounded so mystified, like she truly wanted to know. I had an urge to shake her and tell her she was totally deluded if she thought I'd be safer with Billy than alone, but I just said, "I don't know."

Her mouth crumpled and she pressed her hands to her face, which was greasy with cold cream. "What do you mean you don't know? He was in charge of you, and he just left you! You could have gotten lost. Or kidnapped!"

"Mom." I shook my machete and my bag of candy at her. "It's fine. I'm fine. I mean, have you seen this place? Nobody even locks their bikes!"

She was still looking at me in wounded confusion, like she didn't understand anything about me.

I stared back at her, and she seemed so timid and so small. It made me want to throw down my mask and my candy and shove her as hard as I could. And it made me want to do anything I could to keep her safe and happy and never let her spend a single minute out in the real world.

Neil had stayed ominously quiet, but now he drew himself up and took a step forward so he had Billy trapped against the wall. "I'm curious to know where you learned to be so disobedient."

Billy stared back at him. He was standing with his chin down and his jacket open, looking mutinous. He smelled like beer and the dry-skunk smell of Nate's brother, Silas, and all the other eighth-grade boys who got stoned behind the baseball diamond back home. It was the smell of not caring. "Bite me, Neil. I'm not in the mood."

My mom and I both tensed and moved closer to each other. Usually Billy kept it under control at home. He might have been a total jerk the rest of the time, but he never talked to Neil like that.

For a second, they just stood looking at each other.

Then Neil spoke in a low, dangerous voice. The air was heavy and metallic, like right before a thunderstorm. "I don't know where you've been or what you've been up to, but you will show me some *respect*!"

He shouted the last part. His voice sounded much too big in the smallness of the living room, and I winced, even though I was willing myself not to.

My mom clasped her hands to her collarbone, clutching

the lace on her nightgown, but her expression was already flattening, eyes sliding out of focus like she was slipping out of her own body. I knew what happened next. She would flinch and gasp and look away, but she wouldn't do anything to stop it.

I picked up my machete and put the mask back on. Then I turned and walked back down the hall to my room.

Safe on the other side of my door, I shoved my flannel blanket against the crack at the bottom. It made the shouting quieter, a little.

I dumped out all my candy in the middle of the floor and sat with my back against the footboard of my bed, counting the different kinds and sorting it into piles. Snickers with Snickers, SweeTarts with SweeTarts. The stalker boys had been right. The haul from Loch Nora was excellent. Inside the mask, my face felt hot and slick from my own breath.

Out in the living room, Neil was tuning up. For a while, it was just a rumble of voices, softer sometimes, then louder. There was a short, sharp cry and then a flat, meaty sound, like punching the pocket of a baseball glove.

I pretended it was nothing and I was someplace else. Sitting on the floor of my dad's apartment, maybe, watching *The A-Team*. In a minute the buzzer would sound, and the guy from Little Caesars would be standing in the hall. He'd hand over a pizza with peppers, mushrooms, and three kinds of meat. The smell would waft through the whole apartment, and my dad would put away the puzzle he'd been working on. We'd sit on the floor with the pizza between

79

us, eating our slices straight out of the box. I'd pick off the peppers, he'd pick off the mushrooms, and we'd drink Dr Pepper and watch TV until the late-night movie was over and the test pattern came on. I closed my eyes, and I could almost pretend it was true.

From the other side of the wall, there was the sound of something falling over, but I couldn't tell if it was furniture or a person.

Inside the mask, I was no one, blank as an empty window. Billy seemed faraway, someone I didn't even know.

That's what I told myself, at least—and that he was a jerk. I didn't have to worry about him and his stupid life and his mean, awful dad.

But the truth was worse and more complicated. I did know him. I couldn't help it—I'd been watching him too closely and too long not to.

I repeated the lie anyway, like if I said it with enough force and enough times, I could make myself stop caring.

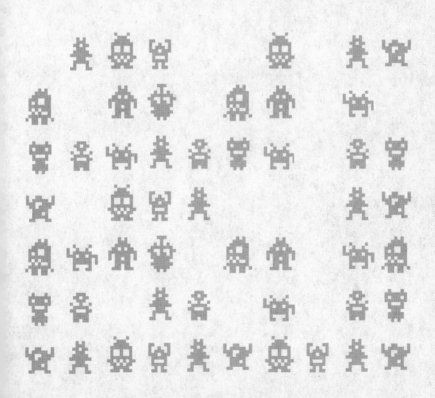

CHAPTER SEVEN

As I got out of the Camaro on Thursday and skated up toward the middle school, I was feeling more optimistic than I had since we'd come to Hawkins. The scene last night had been pretty bad, but now it was morning and I was ready for class, armed with Halloween candy and the idea that maybe I was actually going to like it here. I pushed through the double doors, squeezing past a pair of girls dressed in heavy knit sweater vests and eating a handful of M&M's.

I made it to my locker before the bell and was putting away my board when Lucas showed up. He was alone this time, wearing his normal clothes and looking awkward.

I raised my eyebrows. "Hey, stalker."

The look he gave me was impatient and a little embarrassed, but he didn't argue. He seemed fidgety, though, like he had something else on his mind. Just then, the warning chime rang. I shut my locker and we started for science class together.

It felt weird to be walking down the hall with a boy. A nice boy, with a wide, earnest smile and clean hands. I wasn't going to be all giddy and ridiculous about it, though. Back home, I was always hanging around the halls with Nate, or else Ben and Eddie.

Walking with Lucas felt different. He kept glancing over at me, and it took him a minute to get to what he wanted to say. I thought maybe he was going to tell me why Mike had such a huge problem with me—but it turned out he was mostly just worried about what I thought about Will having a breakdown. The way Lucas was acting, it was like he thought I would freak out about it. That wasn't really my style, though. Sure, I was mouthy sometimes, but I wasn't going to tease Will or go around telling everyone. There were just certain situations where it was better not to be a jerk.

Still, I'd heard things. In the two days I'd been there, it was pretty clear that if there was a Weird Kid in the class, Will was it. Hell, I was the new girl, and I still wasn't even the most interesting thing at Hawkins Middle.

The things people said about him were stupid or ridiculous and totally all over the place. A girl in my history class named Jennifer Mack had said that last fall his mom had reported him missing because he'd been lost in the woods, and it took him forever to find his way back. In my PE class, the general consensus was that his dad had kidnapped him for a week, and some of the boys in English had been elbowing each other and drawing cartoons of him with X's for eyes. They said he'd come back from the dead, which really didn't explain why they were being such jerks, because you'd think if they actually believed that, they'd be nicer about it. It seemed like a bad idea to make fun of a person who'd been raised from the dead, since he was clearly some kind of superhero.

Lucas was looking at me in a hard, unhappy way, like he was trying to make me understand something but couldn't say the words out loud. His breath smelled like Skittles.

His version of the story was pretty much the same as Jennifer Mack's, except he actually knew the details. He said the reason that everyone at school called Will zombie boy was because the whole town had thought he was dead—they'd had a funeral and everything—but his explanation wasn't really doing it for me. Even if Will had really been gone for as long as everyone was saying, a week was way too soon for a funeral. Even if you were searching for someone, getting scared that you might never find them, wouldn't you still try to convince yourself they were missing way before you'd assume that they were dead?

In science, I sat at my desk and stared at the back of Will's head, trying to see him the way Lucas did. Even without really talking to him, I knew the type. He was exactly the kind of boy that other boys always made fun of. It was one of the ways that he reminded me of Nate.

The idea of him as some kind of undead monster was so ridiculous it was actually a little scary, like the twist ending to a story. I'd learned from movies like *Psycho* that sometimes people were dangerous even when they didn't look like it. No matter how hard I stared at Will, he just looked tired and shy and a little bit worried.

Dustin wasn't in his seat, and I figured maybe he'd decided to ditch first hour to sleep in, or else hang around watching reruns and eating Halloween candy.

I was wrong.

He came barreling in late, flustered and out of breath. When I'd come in late on the first day, it had given me a tight, squirmy feeling when everyone turned to look at me. But he didn't seem to care. He flopped down at his desk, totally unfazed by the scene he was making. He ignored Mr. Clarke, leaning across the aisle to whisper to the other stalker boys in the noisiest, most obvious way. Like they had some kind of force field around them, and no one else could see them there. Even when Mr. Clarke finally got annoyed and told him to pay attention, he barely acted like it mattered.

I watched from the back of the room, trying not to feel left out. Dustin was still leaning sideways in his seat, whispering excitedly at Lucas, Mike, and Will. Then he turned to me and mouthed the words *A/V club. Lunch.*

I desperately wanted to know what was going on, but after the whole scene with Will the night before, I was still highly aware that I didn't really know them at all, and maybe they didn't want to know me. I'd come to school that morning half-ready to spend another lunch hour watching the girls over on the four-square grid and messing around on my skateboard. I'd resigned myself to lunch alone with a tuna sandwich and a handful of fun-size Charleston Chews, and it still felt hard to believe I might have found friends in a place like Hawkins.

But the way Dustin had turned and mouthed the words at me was so effortless, and I was ready to spend my lunch someplace that wasn't sitting alone on the steps behind the gym.

• • •

The A/V room was dim and cluttered, all shelves and no windows, more like a closet than a room. There was a big desk in the middle, stacked with loose papers and a computer and a ham radio, and the walls were lined with cubbies full of cords and microphones. It had a stuffy, adult feeling, like it was off-limits to students, but you could tell from how casually the boys let themselves in that they spent a lot of time there.

Dustin was standing at the desk, bent over the ghost trap he'd made for his Halloween costume. It had a pair of mechanical doors that opened on a hinge and were striped with electrical tape. The only thing I knew about why we were there was that he wanted to show us some weird animal he found in the trash on Halloween and then carried to school in the ghost trap for safekeeping. The rest of them were gathered around Dustin, and I squeezed in too.

The ghost trap wasn't like a real trap that you could catch anything with, but it still had a little switch to work the hatch, and he pressed it.

The thing inside was gross and kind of amazing. It was wriggling around in the bottom of the trap like a fat, blind tadpole, only it was about the size of a hamster and covered in slime. I'd heard of rescuing kittens out of dumpsters, but this was on a whole different level.

For a second, we all stood in silence, looking at it. It gave me an uneasy feeling. I wasn't scared of animals—even the creepy-crawly ones. I'd hunted for snakes in the weeds behind my house. Snakes were dry and scaly, though, and even kind of graceful. The thing in Dustin's trap was slippery and lumpy like snot.

Its body was basically a blob, with a pointed tail and two stubby little front legs. Dustin scooped it out of the trap, and I squinted at it, studying its bulbous head. I was looking for the eyes, because it didn't seem to have them. I'd never seen anything like it.

Dustin bent over the table, gazing at the creature in his hands like it was the sweetest, most adorable thing. He kept calling it a *he,* even though it was so weird and shapeless that how could you tell?

When he saw me staring, he asked if I wanted to hold it, and I shook my head, but he turned and tipped it out of his cupped palms and into mine.

It felt cool and squishy, heavier than it looked, and I passed it to Lucas fast. Lucas handed it off to Will, and it made its way around the circle. I was a little relieved to see that I wasn't the only one shrinking back from it. Will was looking at it like it had some kind of disease, and even Mike didn't exactly seem thrilled to touch it. He was the bravest, though, and held it up for a closer look.

The way Dustin was so excited about a giant tadpole was a little intense. He was telling us all kinds of random trivia— that it was a terrestrial pollywog and he'd named it Dart and it liked 3 Musketeers bars but hated light. The whole thing was totally bizarre, like a big, complicated game, and I wasn't sure I was even really part of it.

Still, it was fun to watch Dustin leaf through a stack of books about amphibians that he'd brought from the library, and it was nice to have something be fun and exciting again. It had been months since I'd had a chance to be part of something.

The way Will had stared at the tadpole, so tense and wary, was weird. I wasn't planning to cuddle it or anything, but it wasn't actually scary. It was just gross and a little slimy, small enough to hold in your hand. He was watching it like he was frozen, and I wondered again if this was turning out to be some kind of real-life *Dungeons and Dragons*, but he didn't seem like he was pretending.

After lunch, we headed to class. Dustin was on a whole big thing about how he'd discovered a new species, how he was going to name it after himself, and what he was going to do when he was famous. I listened, but it still sort of felt like we were playing a game. Or else they were playing a game, and I just happened to be hanging around with them while they did it, I just didn't know the rules.

I went along with it anyway. Dustin was so excited about the tadpole, it was almost cute. And even though the whole thing was kind of dorky, it wasn't like we hadn't had our own games at home.

Back in San Diego we'd hung out in the hills behind my house every day after school and run wild there all summer. Even before I learned to skateboard, I was in love with how it felt to ride fast and reckless on the back of Nate's BMX, balanced there with my hands on his shoulders and my feet on the pegs. We zoomed down Wakeland Road with our eyes closed, the wind against our faces. We took our feet off the pedals and let go of the handlebars and never cared how many times we wiped out.

When I thought about the life I'd left behind in California, it felt bright and faraway, almost like a dream. I kept catching myself turning nostalgic for it, remembering the very best parts—afternoons at the go-kart track or the beach. Summer nights looking for toads in the warm, dusky silence of Eddie's mom's garden.

The Harrises' house was a pretty little bungalow with morning glories growing over the gate and toads that hopped clumsily across winding stone paths. We chased them through the rosebushes and caught them in an old colander. We always had this big plan to name them and keep them as pets, even though they smelled like fish guts, and half the time they peed all over your hands when you picked them up. We put them in a cereal box and fed them crickets until we got bored and they got mad. Then we'd let them go again under the roses.

The garden was as big as an Olympic swimming pool—bigger than my whole yard—but we didn't hang out there very much because Eddie's mom was always buzzing around after us, making trays of celery with peanut butter and handing out napkins. It was annoying and a little weird to have a grown-up actually pay attention to what we did.

The rest of us had parents who never seemed to notice we existed. Nate's mom spent the afternoons slumped in front of the TV, and Ben's dad dropped us off at the rec center or the roller rink sometimes but was usually too busy running his roofing business or rebuilding the dune buggy that was sitting out in his driveway. My mom was less checked-out and definitely more functional than Nate's, but she never came out to the ditch behind the house.

We lived our daily lives in places where no one would

poke their head in and want to know what we were up to, but on nights when the smog was down and the moon was up, we would all go over to Eddie's. We'd sit cross-legged under the roses or lie on the little strip of lawn between the flower beds and the house, looking up at the night sky, breathing the warm, dizzying smell of the flowers.

We didn't pretend things, because we didn't need to. Our games and inventions were actually real. When we built machines, they worked. And when we wanted something to feel magical, all we had to do was lie in the Harrises' garden and look up.

• • •

As the last bell rang, turning us loose for the day, I was feeling pretty good, bouncing along on the thought of spending an afternoon with friends. I had an idea that maybe I'd even go out to the parking lot and tell Billy I didn't need a ride.

Then reality sank in, and I lost some of the bounce. When you started counting on other people to include you, or started assuming you had after-school plans without having to check, that was a danger zone. There was no point in getting excited about something that wasn't even real.

As I stopped by my locker to drop off my math book and pick up my skateboard and my backpack, I reminded myself that even though Lucas and Dustin had been friendly, I shouldn't count on them too much. After all, at home my social life had been built on seven years of schemes and projects and adventures. And in the end, it had turned out that even the friends I thought would always have my back . . . didn't.

"Hey, Max!"

I turned, tucking my skateboard under my arm. It was Lucas.

For a second, I could hear Billy somewhere in a dingy corner of my mind, telling me that Lucas was going to get bored with me. He would forget about me, just like my friends at home had forgotten about me, because I was that much of a drag. It was stupid to think that because we went trick-or-treating once, they'd want me around the rest of the time. I was this weird, unlikable girl, and no one wanted to hang around with the weird girl. I told myself all that, in Billy's low, flat voice because it felt truer than using my own. Billy could be out of control and was a total jerk, but he was usually right.

Lucas was standing in front of me, looking expectant. He smiled, and Billy's voice was interrupted by the voice of my better self. *Stop it, Max.*

Lucas didn't seem like the type to be friendly in a just-being-polite way, and it was pretty obvious that he was going out of his way to find me. If he was inviting me along, it was because he wanted to, not just because he was checking up or worried what I would tell the other kids in our grade about them. For one thing, their secrets just weren't that interesting. And anyway, I didn't talk to any of the other kids.

Lucas had stopped smiling, but his gaze was easy and direct. He made a *hurry up* gesture. "Come on, we're taking Dart to show Mr. Clarke."

When Dustin said anything to me, it was always more like he was talking *at* me, like he was mostly worried about how to make himself seem interesting or impressive. I kind of got the feeling that he wasn't actually thinking about much at all. Whereas Lucas sounded less fawning and more impatient. His voice was low and abrupt and a little hoarse. I liked that. My mom was always so sensitive about how people spoke to her, like the tone was all that mattered. They could be saying the most awful things in the sweetest voice and she would melt for it. But even when Lucas sounded irritable or impatient, I didn't mind. He never seemed like he was trying to talk me into anything.

I shoved my homework into my backpack and slammed my locker door. "What's Mr. Clarke supposed to do about it? Is he some kind of tadpole expert?"

Lucas shrugged. He didn't seem bothered that I never knew how to sound soft. His eyes were dark and steady, like I was someone worth learning about.

I thought I might have the same way of watching things, a little. My mom was always telling me to stop giving her that bug-eyed look. She said the way I stared at people, it was like I was trying to pull them apart piece by piece.

Lucas looked at people too, but he did it in a level, intent way, like he was just trying to see. He looked thoughtful, not hostile, and when he smiled, it was wide and sheepish.

It had been forever since it felt like someone was actually going out of their way to try to see me.

"Come on," he said again, and I followed him.

In Mr. Clarke's room, we stood in a little circle around the desk as Dustin got ready to take Dart out of the ghost trap.

I was pretty interested to see what Mr. Clarke thought. Maybe he was an expert on giant slimy tadpoles? Dustin was taking his time about revealing Dart, though, making a production out of it.

We were all watching in anticipation when Mike came sprinting in. He was wide-eyed and breathing hard. Without any warning or explanation, he grabbed the trap out of Dustin's hands and shouted to Mr. Clarke that the whole thing was just a dumb prank. Then he took off, bolting out of the room with Dart and the ghost trap, leaving Mr. Clarke looking totally baffled.

Lucas and Dustin only hesitated a second before chasing after him. After a beat, I shrugged and followed them.

Back at the A/V room, they all crammed inside, but Mike stopped in the doorway. I went to push past him, and he stepped in front of me, blocking my way.

"Not you." Then he turned and shut the door in my face.

I heard the lock click, and then I was alone in the hall.

For a second, I just stood there, staring at the closed door. I was getting used to Mike's moodiness, but this was ridiculous. Apparently, I was allowed to tag along after them, but not to be in on any of their plans or secrets. I dropped my backpack, still hearing the echo of Mike's voice: *Not you.*

After pounding on the door for a minute, I sat out in the hall on my board. I thought about starting on my homework, but it was hard to concentrate knowing that I was being left out, and that even though Dustin and Lucas were friendly enough to me when we were eating lunch or messing around during the passing periods, they were still totally on board with Mike when it came to keeping me out.

I could trade fun-size Snickers for Clark Bars and walk to class with Lucas or Dustin, but as soon as their party was all together, I wasn't part of the game.

And maybe it wasn't fair to expect them to just scoot over and make room for me, but it wasn't fair to invite me into the party and then kick me out again whenever they felt like it. I didn't have to stick around and keep trying to earn my way in. I could go home or head downtown to the arcade and play *Dig Dug,* whatever I wanted. Nothing was keeping me there.

I waited anyway.

The truth was, I still had a small, stupid hope that maybe after they were through with whatever covert business they were up to, we'd all hang out together. And even more than that, I wanted to know what was happening in the A/V room. I was more and more curious how that blind, slimy tadpole had turned into some huge secret.

The hall was empty. All the other kids had gone home, and most of the teachers were grading papers in their classrooms or making copies in the front office. The whole place had taken on a spooky, abandoned feeling.

I'd only been sitting there for a few minutes when I got the uneasy feeling that something was happening. The door to the A/V room wasn't soundproof, and I didn't even have to put my ear against it to hear the noises coming from inside.

At first, it sounded like the normal scuffling sounds of boys arguing over comic books or baseball cards, and I didn't think too much about it. Then I heard Lucas say something in a tense, irritable voice, and there was a commotion of banging and thumping.

I reached into my backpack and grabbed a paper clip. My dad was always telling me that you should never go any-where without the tools to pick a padlock or a doorknob. I straightened the paper clip in a fast, fluid jerk, even though part of me was still whispering that maybe this was all just a game.

The noises on the other side of the door were mak-ing me nervous, though. I jammed the paper clip into the doorknob and felt around for the tumbler. From inside the A/V room came a whole bunch of chirps and squeals, and someone yelled. It sounded like Lucas.

There was a loose rattle, then a click, and I held the paper clip steady and turned the handle.

As soon as the door swung open, something came scram-bling out with the boys all flailing after it. Lucas tripped and went sprawling next to me, but Dustin crashed straight into me, and we both landed in a tangled heap on the hall floor.

I looked around wildly. "What *is* that?"

Mike stood over us, his eyes wide in exasperation and alarm. "Dart! You let him escape!"

I stared up at him. I'd had just enough time to register the shape of the creature as it bolted from the A/V room. It had squat, froggy legs and a huge, yawning mouth, and it looked hardly anything like the lumpy blind tadpole Dustin had showed us this morning. It had squirted past me down the hall, feet paddling frantically on the linoleum. And now it was gone.

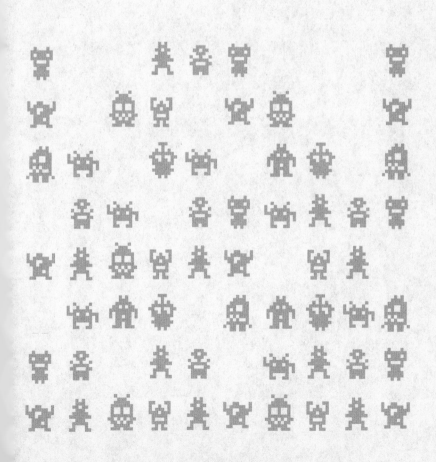

CHAPTER EIGHT

The hall stretched empty in both directions. Dart was nowhere.

The boys decided that we should spread out to search the school. As we all headed off in different directions, I had a sinking feeling that I had ruined whatever chance with them I might have had.

I made my way through the athletics hall, checking the classrooms and the equipment closets. I didn't want to feel bad about Dart. If they hadn't locked me out of the A/V room, none of this would have happened. But I had a guilty feeling that I needed to fix it anyway. It didn't matter whose fault it was; I was still the one who'd let him out.

I was poking around in the locker rooms off the side of the gym, searching through empty lockers and trash cans, when there was a howl and someone leapt out behind me.

I whirled around, but it was only Mike, waving a mop and staring at me like I'd done something offensive just by being there. I figured now that it was only the two of us, we'd have to talk about the awful way he kept treating me, but he just turned and walked away from me, back out into the gym.

I wasn't about to let it drop, though, and I followed him.

"Why do you hate me so much?" I said it in a hard, matter-of-fact way.

It was the kind of question you weren't supposed to ask, but I'd learned that sometimes you could get a straight answer just by being more up front than the other person. I'd never had a problem telling the truth, but some people didn't like to say things if they thought it was going to make you mad. So being direct was the easiest way of dealing with them. Like, for example, sometimes it was the only way to get a straight answer from my mom.

Mike glanced quickly over his shoulder without really looking at me. "I don't hate you."

The way he said it was clipped and stony, and I didn't want to believe it, because the alternative was that he was telling the truth and just treating me terribly anyway.

• • •

For pretty much my whole life, I'd been really bad at talking to people. It wasn't because I was nervous or shy. I didn't worry about being bullied or worry that no one would think I was cool, but the idea of me actually being popular was absurd. I didn't know how to make people *like* me.

It should have been easy, or at least doable. My dad made friends with everyone, like making friends wasn't even something you had to *do*. More like it was a commonplace natural element, waiting for him as soon as he walked into a room, easy as breathing.

Anywhere we went, he collected people. It was like his superpower. I mostly just made them want to strangle me.

It was one of the visitation weekends right after the divorce, back when I still got to see him twice a month. For two days, we'd been hanging around the apartment. He'd been running a little sports-betting thing on the side and had spent all of Sunday afternoon sitting at the counter, calculating point spreads and who owed him money, while I flipped through the same four channels on TV over and over and messed around with my skateboard. But now it was getting dark, and I was starving.

"There's no food," I said, opening the refrigerator and staring inside.

Even on the thinnest days, there were usually a few baloney slices or a carton of leftover Chinese food, but now the shelves were bare. I sighed and shut the door. There wasn't anything sadder than a refrigerator with nothing inside except a naked yellow lightbulb and a jar of relish with rust and black stuff caked on the lid.

So my dad took me down the block to the Black Door Lounge and bought me a hot ham and cheese. I ate it while he talked to some of the scuzzy guys in the back, taking bets on the Dodgers game and playing a few rounds of pool.

Everyone at the Black Door loved him. As soon as we walked in, they would all shift around on their stools and clamor for his attention. That was how it was everywhere— a crowd of people falling all over themselves, shouting *Sam! How you been?* and slapping him on the back. He was good at the kind of teasing that people liked. Whenever I tried it, I just sounded harsh and confrontational.

That night, he was in a big, expansive mood. He made his way toward the back, grinning and high-fiving, while I trailed along behind him trying to look invisible so no one would ask me when I was going to learn how to hustle darts like my dad and how old I was now and whether I had any boyfriends yet.

My dad always let me tag along with him and treated me like his coolest, proudest thing, but I wasn't slick or friendly like he was, and I had no idea how to fake it. The way he could just slide into a room and make everyone love him was like a magic trick. I didn't get it. My mom always said that he could charm the spots off a ladybug. I couldn't even order fries or ask for directions without sounding like I was about to take hostages.

The hot ham and cheese was greasy and not very hot.

I sat at the end of the bar with a basket of fries and a glass of Coke on a paper napkin, practicing on the little padlock from a pink patent leather diary my mom had given me. It was a cheat: the lock was so easy you could pick it with the end of a ballpoint pen, and the strap that held it to the diary was flimsy enough that you could probably just peel it off.

I was popping the shackle for the third time when a leathery-tan woman in a sequined top crossed the lounge and sank onto the seat next to me.

"What a cute little diary," she said, leaning close so that the stiff bird's nest of her hair brushed my arm. I could smell beer and honey-roasted peanuts on her breath. "A lot of secrets in there?"

I hunched over the book and shook my head. When I twisted the paper clip, it made a soft *snick,* and the lock popped open.

The woman fumbled a lighter out of her purse and lit a cigarette. She was watching me in bleary curiosity, with her elbows on the bar, letting her drink dangle from her hand. The glass was half-full of something dark brown and decorated with a pair of cherries on a plastic sword. I wondered if I could figure out a way to pick the diary lock with a cocktail sword, then decided it would probably break. And anyway, I didn't want to ask the woman for hers.

She was leaning on the bar, staring at the side of my face, and I tried not to look at her. I wanted to tell her to buzz off, but I'd already spent enough time in bars to know not to argue with drunk people. It never went anywhere good.

She downed the rest of her drink in a long swallow and reached over my arm to grab the book. I tried to tug it away from her, but I didn't feel like getting into a wrestling match over it, and in the end, I let her have it.

"Let's have a look," she said in a bright voice, pronouncing all the words too clearly, the way drunk people did when they wanted to sound sober. She was wearing so much makeup it was caking in the creases around her eyes.

Then she leaned back on the stool, holding the diary above her head. "We're having a dramatic reading," she called, looking around the bar. She didn't wait for anyone to answer, just slid clumsily off the stool and turned to face the lounge.

The rest of the regulars glanced at her. They all looked deeply bored. There were a few snickers, but most of the guys at the pool tables were completely uninterested in whatever pink, girly thing we were doing.

I sat on the stool with my chin stuck out. My mouth felt angry and small. The woman was trying to make a spectacle of me, and I had to remind myself that it didn't really matter. She opened the diary and held it up in front of her like she was about to recite a speech in a school play. Then she stood there with her mouth open and her cigarette smoldering in her free hand.

The book was blank, of course.

My dad was watching from the back pool table, and he smiled at me. He didn't put down his pool cue or say anything, but the way he was smirking made me smirk a little too. I was Sam Mayfield's daughter, and maybe we liked our word games and puzzles and notes in code, but that was as far as it went. His rules were simple: you never showed your hand, you never gave away your time or your talents, and you never wrote down your secrets.

The woman lowered her head and handed me the diary. With a heavy, phlegmy sigh, she sank back onto the stool, like looking stupid in front of a bunch of barflies who didn't even care was somehow my fault.

It was disgusting, the way people always wanted to embarrass girls or tease them about their feelings. Like the very fact of having something that you cared about was worth laughing at. They all wanted me to be this certain soft frilly way, just so they could make fun of me.

The woman mashed out her cigarette in the bottom of her empty glass. There was so much lipstick on the filter, you'd have thought her mouth was bleeding.

She gave me a long, baleful look. Her face seemed saggy and tired. "I guess you think that's pretty cute."

I shrugged and kept my expression blank, but my skull felt hot behind my eyes. I hated that I was supposed to be her punch line. "No, I think it's pretty smart."

. . .

In the gym, Mike stalked away from me like he had someplace to be, but I could tell he was just trying to avoid looking at me. I followed him. I already knew I wouldn't be able to win him over the same way my dad would, though. My dad was a pro when it came to lightening the mood. He never had to ask people why they hated him.

Mike was stomping around like he had some personal grudge against me. Even if he didn't hate me, he was still acting like I'd ruined his life, and I wasn't letting him leave without an explanation. "Yeah, but you don't want me in your party."

He spun around to face me. "Correct!"

"Why *not*?"

"Because you're annoying!"

He said it in a hard, exasperated voice, like that would be enough to hurt my feelings or make me back off. Like I was so sensitive and delicate that being called annoying was the worst thing anyone could say to me, when I had to live with Billy every day.

I hadn't expected it, though. It left a raw ache in my chest, but I stared back and got my face under control. At least we were getting somewhere.

He was on a roll now, listing all the ways they didn't need me, how every one of them belonged to the group and had a purpose and I didn't. The stuff he was telling me wasn't real, just all this fantasy role-playing about paladins and clerics. Then he said something that made no sense at all. "El was our Mage."

When he said it, something happened on his face that I didn't understand. There was no one else, no fifth party member, and it took me a second to really get that he was talking about someone who was gone.

He went on, trying to seem like he was bored and above it all, but I knew what he was *really* saying. I was being shut out by the memory of this other person, this girl who was on the inside of the circle and knew secrets I didn't. A girl who wasn't *annoying*. Who didn't take up too much space or say the wrong thing. Who wasn't even around anymore. All he was saying was that I wasn't allowed to be part of the group because once there'd been another girl. A better girl.

He was looking down, like he was trying to tell a story but didn't know what words to use, or maybe he was just embarrassed by how it felt to say them out loud. It was a story that was obviously important to him, but the parts he was saying didn't mean anything to me, and I had to bite back the jab that kept forming inside my mouth.

Hearing someone's most important thing was a little too much like seeing them without their skin. Sometimes the total unguardedness of it made me want to be mean. I had a quick, unhappy anger in me that made me feel like the woman at the Black Door trying to embarrass me over the possibility that I might have feelings. I didn't want to hurt him. It was what Billy would have done, and I wanted to be better than that. It was just so hard to be gentle when you knew someone's weaknesses.

Instead, I followed him through the gym on my board, gliding across the basketball court. When I coasted around him in lazy circles, with my arms held out, he smiled, even though it looked tense and he was trying to act like he wasn't. The gym floor was polished to a buttery shine, and it slipped like grease under my wheels. I was showing off, but sometimes you had to show off to get boys to see you as a real person and not just *another girl*. I needed him to stop acting like I was somehow stepping on the memory of a girl I'd never met.

He was watching me as I cruised past, laughing even though he looked a little like he was still trying not to, when something strange happened.

There was a heavy feeling in my chest, like the air had gotten thicker. The board jerked out from under me as suddenly as if someone had grabbed the nose and pulled.

I hit the basketball court with a thud that made my ears ring. The impact echoed through my ribs.

Mike stood over me, looking puzzled. He held out his hand and reached to help me up. "Are you okay?"

I nodded, holding my side where I'd landed. I was looking past him, toward the doors—there was nothing there. I started back across the gym for my board, trying to shake the eerie, creeping feeling that someone had touched me.

But the place was empty. It was just the two of us.

CHAPTER NINE

The next morning, I woke up with a bruise down my side where I'd fallen and a strange, unsteady feeling that everything was changing. I just didn't know what it was changing into.

Yesterday afternoon had been wild. After Mike had finally started being honest with me in the gym, we'd had to accept the fact that Dart was nowhere. The search had been cut short anyway, because as soon as Mike helped me up and we left the gym, Will had had another episode. He'd been standing out in the field behind the school, pale and rigid, when his mom showed up to get him.

She was small in stature, with dark hair and a worried

face, and I recognized her as the woman from the afternoon downtown when I'd wiped out on my board and she'd run out to see if I was okay.

She'd understood right away what was happening with Will, and after he finally came back to himself, she took him home.

The way the rest of them acted when we found him out there was weird—like they were frightened for him but not particularly shocked. Almost like they'd been expecting it. I was a little surprised that he was still allowed to come to school if he was in such bad shape. I figured it was like Jamie Winslow in my class at home. She had one of those rare kid-cancers and had to wear a wig. She still came to school when she could, and I figured even when they were in bad shape, sometimes people just wanted to feel normal.

After we'd called off the search for Dart, everyone went their separate ways.

It was no surprise when I got out to the parking lot and Billy was gone. And the next morning, he left without giving me a ride to school. He said it was because he had to be there early for some basketball thing. I knew he was still trying to punish me for making him wait, though. I didn't care how long the walk was. It was still better than being trapped in the car with him.

Mike and Lucas were standing around out front when I got there. I'd expected they'd want to hang out in the A/V room again, but they said they were waiting for Dustin so they could search for Dart some more. We started without him, digging around in the dumpster by the back steps, in case Dart had magically decided to make his way back to the habitat he'd been living in when Dustin found him. I was pretty sure we weren't going to have much luck, but we searched anyway, hauling out the trash and going through it with a couple of old mop handles.

I still wasn't sure why Dart was such a big deal, but they were bent on finding him, and since I was the one who'd let him out, the least I could do was help look for him.

I could see how someone would be upset about losing an important discovery, and if your pet went missing, you'd definitely want it back. But their level of concern for a mutant frog was a little bizarre—showing up to school early, rooting around in a dumpster—and I wondered what they'd been talking about when they locked me out of the A/V room. They still wouldn't say what was so special about him. No matter how you looked at it, though, when Dart had escaped, I'd seen a pair of back legs when he hadn't had them just a few hours before. In less than a day, he'd grown a whole new set of body parts, and that definitely wasn't normal.

Will wasn't at school, and the boys were anxious and preoccupied. Still, things seemed to be going okay, right up until lunch.

We were sitting out on the steps, eating our sandwiches and talking about how they did the ectoplasm effects in

Ghostbusters. Mike had gone to use the pay phone to call Will's house; then all of a sudden he came running back, yelling that we needed to talk right away in the A/V room.

Lucas and Dustin both jumped up, and the three of them headed inside. When I tried to follow, though, Mike turned and gave me an exasperated look. "Party members *only*."

It wasn't as if I'd thought that our stupid heart-to-heart in the gym made us best friends, or that now Mike was suddenly going to welcome me with open arms, but I'd thought we'd maybe worked out some kind of truce.

Lucas and Dustin both acted embarrassed, like they felt bad about it, but a few muttered *sorry*s weren't enough to make up for the way they hadn't stuck up for me.

I'd been loyal to the party, even though I didn't understand half of what was happening. I hadn't told anyone about Will's latest episode, or their stupid missing frog, or even asked about their missing Mage. I dug around in trash for them.

That afternoon was long and dismal. In history, we were studying for a quiz to name all the presidents in order, but I didn't pay much attention. I'd already had to memorize them last year.

When I asked the girl next to me if I could borrow her eraser, she looked right past me like I was nowhere, like I was a person-shaped hole and she was looking through me.

The way I could disappear while I was still standing in a room reminded me of things I tried not to think about.

The way my mom and dad had just decided to stop loving each other and pass me between them like a spare garden hose or lug wrench. Except, even that had changed. First with Neil, and then with the move. Instead of being able to count on a trip to my dad's every couple of weeks, what used to be an agreement had turned into my mom wanting to keep me away from the one person who actually understood me.

Sure, there were things that weren't so great. Although my dad was usually pretty good with commitments and schedules (when he tried), sometimes he'd get all excited about me coming up from San Diego and start making plans to change out the wheels on my board or promise to take me to Knott's Berry Farm. Then he'd get so distracted drinking beer and working on one of his side gigs that he'd lose track of time, and we'd wind up just sitting around his apartment all weekend.

Later he'd always be sorry, but letting me pick the horses for him at the track wasn't really an apology. It never made up for the feeling that I was ignorable, forgettable. Unnecessary.

After school, I was dropping off my books and collecting my skateboard when I was interrupted by the sound of Lucas calling my name. I closed my locker and walked out of the school without looking at him.

The doors wheezed shut behind me and he followed me, but I was done with the way he thought he could just keep pretending he was my friend without ever bothering to include me or explain anything.

When he caught up to me in the parking lot, I spun around and lit into him. Here he was, acting like I was the one who was being totally unreasonable, and I wasn't going to just smile and nod and stand there for it.

Lucas spread his hands and blurted out a parade of excuses: It wasn't like that. They did want me around, but it was just too complicated to talk about. There were things they couldn't tell me, for my own safety.

That last one was so ridiculous I couldn't keep the incredulity off my face.

"My own *safety*?" My voice spiked in disbelief. What he was saying had no bearing on anything about my actual life. "Because I'm a girl?"

He stared back, shaking his head, but he had no real answers for me. I was just supposed to believe all his vague secrecy and stop asking questions. The idea that he could protect me from anything was ridiculous. If he actually believed that, it just proved that he didn't know the first thing about my life or what I needed. It was infuriating that someone was trying to save me from things I didn't need to be saved from.

Billy was waiting for me down in the senior lot. There were so many things that no one in my life had ever protected me from.

• • •

My mom was basically useless when it came to being fierce or protective. I'd read that mother wolves and bears and lions would mess you up if you came near their cubs, but she didn't have that instinct. She was always mousing around or apologizing, acting like she didn't know what was happening in our house.

Sometimes, though, she had an eye for things I didn't. Sometimes she took me by surprise.

The garage at home in San Diego had been attached to the house. It was big enough to park two cars next to each other, even though we never did, and you could get to it from inside through a door at the back of the laundry room.

Billy hung out there a lot, with his friends or by himself. He kept a transistor radio on the workbench and a bench press in the corner. On weekends and afternoons, I'd find him out there in the shade of the open garage with the music blasting, lifting weights or working on his car.

I'd been changing the wheels on my skateboard, and when I went out for an Allen wrench, Billy was in the garage with the door up. He was in his undershirt, working under the hood of the Camaro with a cigarette clamped between his teeth. He'd finally gotten his keys back from Neil.

Before he and Neil moved in, the garage was just where we kept the Christmas lights. My mom mostly parked her car in the driveway, and I never went out there except to look for the Allen wrench—and no one ever smoked. Now there was always a jumbo Folgers can on the corner of the workbench, full of ashes and cigarette butts. Before, I hadn't cared about the garage one way or another, but now I felt weirdly protective, like it was just one more conquered territory in a house that had been mine and wasn't anymore.

I sat on the concrete step with the door to the laundry room open behind me and watched Billy for a while. The hood of the Camaro made an aggressive angle, smoke puffing up from underneath.

I leaned forward with my knees on my elbows and cupped my chin in my hands. "At the health assembly in school, they told us that we're not supposed to smoke."

Billy straightened and closed the hood, wiping his hands with a rag. "And do you always do everything your teachers tell you?"

That idea was so wrong it was hilarious. My grades were usually okay, but my conduct cards were a mess. I was always in trouble for something—talking back, or drawing cartoon hot rods on my desk with a felt pen. I laughed and shook my head.

That seemed to make him happy. He smiled in a slow, lazy way, then pulled the pack of Parliaments out of his shirt pocket. He held it out to me and waited, watching my face until I took one.

I'd never smoked before, and the cigarette felt weird in my hand, but the actual mechanics of it seemed pretty simple. I'd watched Billy plenty of times. I stuck the filter in my mouth and held still while he leaned over and lit it for me.

I sucked in, feeling the first dry billow of smoke, hot in

the back of my throat. It tasted like batteries and burning newspaper, and I coughed so hard my eyes teared up.

Billy was leaning against the Camaro, laughing with his head back and his eyebrows raised, and I was pinching the cigarette awkwardly between my fingers, trying not to choke, when I heard a gasp behind me.

"Maxine!"

My mom only called me that when I was in trouble. She marched down the garage steps and grabbed the cigarette out of my mouth. I'd only taken two or three puffs.

Billy was still leaning against the side of the Camaro laughing, and I had a crazy urge to laugh too, just to show him that I wasn't freaked out by the way the smoke burned the inside of my nose or how red-faced and guilty I must have looked. That I was in on it.

My mom was staring at me in total horror, and I was sure she was going to ground me, but most of her anger seemed to be pointed at Billy.

She turned on him, looking outraged. "Do you think this is funny?"

"Come on, Susan. It's just one cigarette. Relax."

My mom stared at him. *"Relax?"* Her voice was high and furious. "Look, mister! You can fill your lungs with crud or wrap yourself around a telephone pole in that death machine, or whatever else you want to do to yourself, but the party ends there! You are not dragging my daughter down with you!"

It was the first time I'd seen her truly mad in a long time, and I suddenly felt really sorry. I'd only taken the cigarette because it seemed like the cool thing, the obvious thing. I hadn't even considered how my mom would feel about it or what she'd think.

Her mouth was so thin she must have been biting the inside of her lip, and I hoped she wasn't going to cry, the way she sometimes did when she got mad. Her eyes had a wide, wounded look, but her cheeks were a bright, angry red.

Billy had taken out another cigarette, and now he lit it. He was smirking in that bored, insolent way he always did when he was trying to get a rise out of her. The flick of the lighter seemed to break something inside her, and her anger crumbled into helplessness. It was always so easy.

The three of us were standing in the garage when Neil got home. He parked his truck in the driveway and came striding toward the house, then stopped.

He stood in the open garage door, looking tall and face-less with the sun at his back. "What's going on in here?"

We all stood frozen in the shade of the garage, not know-ing what was going to happen next. I braced myself, waiting to see what Neil was going to do. My mom was huddled near the back of the Camaro with her arms folded around herself, and I waited for her to tell him that Billy had given me a cigarette and then talked back to her when she tried to reprimand him. Instead, she just smiled and glanced away like she was nervous.

In front of the Camaro, Billy was standing at attention, looking angry and defiant.

The air felt electric, like the cloud of blue smoke after a firecracker, and it tasted worse. I pressed my lips together to keep myself from coughing and tried to look normal.

My mom dropped the cigarette into the coffee can and shook her head. "Nothing."

Right then, standing in the garage, I hadn't gotten it. I'd thought my mom was too scared of Billy to tell Neil what he'd done. Later, though, once the novelty of having a stepdad had worn off, and I got to know Neil—the real Neil—I understood what my mom must have already known: Sure, she could be nervous and oversensitive, and she apologized too much, but she wasn't dumb. She hadn't been scared of Billy, she'd been scared *for* him.

• • •

There were things I wished I could be kept safe from, but none of them were the kinds of things Lucas could do anything about. The way he seemed to think he could help me by keeping me out gave me a hollow feeling.

Even though I'd been in Indiana for less than a week, I'd been starting to think that things were looking up. That I'd found a place where I fit. I'd done everything I could to make a space for myself, and it still wasn't enough. I was never going to be part of their club.

Even Lucas, who acted like he thought I was cool, and who almost always said what he was actually thinking, wouldn't say the truth about that. Every conversation between them was some hush-hush secret meeting, with me on the outside. I might be good enough to go trick-or-treating or eat lunch with, but I still wasn't one of them.

All week, I'd been twisting myself in knots trying to figure out a way to belong here, but now I understood that it was pointless. Hawkins wasn't some magic solution or an answer to a question, and wide streets and Halloween decorations didn't make it home. There was no place for me in a tiny, sleepy town full of cow pastures and sewing machine repair shops.

My only place was in the passenger seat of that stupid Camaro.

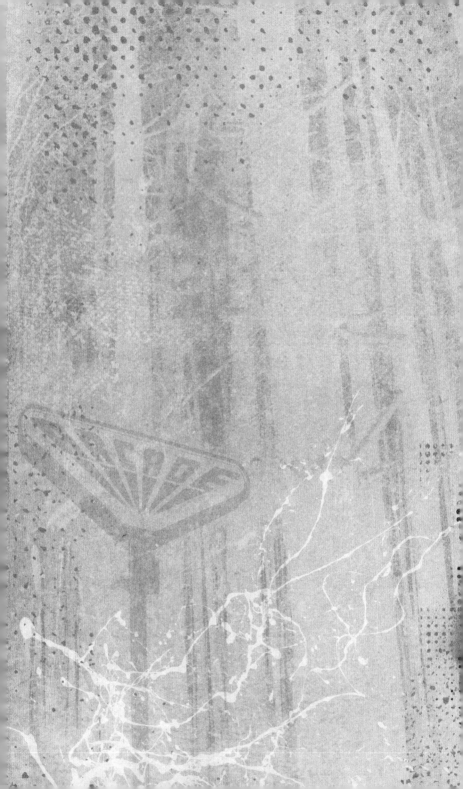

CHAPTER TEN

When I stalked away from Lucas, Billy was waiting for me, leaning against the fender of the Camaro. "That kid you were talking to, who is he?"

"He's no one." I got in and slammed the door.

Billy slid into the driver's seat and lit a cigarette but didn't start the car. He was staring out across the parking lot. "Why was he talking to you?" His voice was dangerously even, and I was gripped by a horrible sinking feeling. I knew what came next. "He causing you trouble?"

"Why do you care?"

"Because, Max, you're a piece of crap, but we're family."

I threw up my hands and rolled my eyes. "Whatever would I do without—"

He reached out fast and caught me by the wrist. "There are people in this world that you stay away from."

He was leaning close, staring right into my face, and he sounded serious and scary. He was acting like he was looking out for me, but I knew what he really meant. We weren't just talking about being friends with boys. Neil—and, I guess, Billy—had a lot of opinions about anybody who wasn't white and Lutheran and a man. Neil said it was just that different kinds of people belonged in different worlds. That it was about property values, or crime, or a million other coded things, so that he didn't have to say what he really meant. People like *that*.

I stuck out my chin and stared back at Billy, but when I tried to jerk away, he held on. His fingers dug into my wrist. After a second, he let me go and started the car.

It pissed me off that he could even act like he had any right to judge a person by looking at them. The way he'd stared after Lucas made me very nervous about what he might do next, but right away, that was canceled out by another thought. I didn't even have to *try* to stay away from Lucas, because that was over now. They didn't want me around. I meant nothing to them. I stared out the window and tried not to cry.

When Billy got mad, it was scary, but I was used to it. The way he could make fun of my hobbies or my friends or call me names was bad sometimes; I mostly tried not to take it personally. It was nothing. It was like the little rhyme we used to sing on the playground about sticks and stones. I could handle it. Yeah, it felt awful, and I hated the way Nate and Ben and Eddie had looked at me sometimes, like they were sorry for me, but there was no other option. I had to handle it.

Sometimes, though, Billy acted like we were in on some big, crucial secret together. Like we understood each other, like he was so worried about me. And that was worse.

I knew he wasn't really worried. He'd just found one more way to mess with me.

. . .

Since their big Halloween blowup two days ago, standing in the living room when Neil and Billy were both there was like standing under power lines—so high-voltage you could hear the hum.

Back in San Diego, they'd been angry with each other, but it had usually stayed under the surface. Now I was starting to understand that it had only been that way because Billy was hardly ever home. Here in Hawkins, he had nothing but time. Since we'd moved into the house on Cherry Road, he'd certainly tried to fill that time with parties and girls and the basketball team. But the girls here all had curfews. And there weren't that many parties and that many places to go.

Neil was in a similar rut, or maybe that was just how

grown-ups always were. He left for work in the mornings and came home after five like always, and when he walked in, he would ruffle my hair or hand my mom some flowers, but underneath, he was like a box of dynamite. I spent my time waiting for the explosion.

It was important to be ready, because if Neil and Billy got into a disagreement, Billy would take it out on me. And if by some miracle the explosion didn't come, he would take it out on me anyway, just to blow off steam.

That morning they'd had a strange, wordless argument over breakfast. Billy had taken the orange juice from the middle of the table, and Neil reached over to take it back, but Billy didn't let go. Neither of them said anything. The carton hovered between them, their hands flexed, fingers digging into the waxed cardboard. Then Neil pulled so hard the carton jerked out of Billy's hand. Neil's elbow swung around and knocked my mom's little red sugar bowl onto the floor. Now the bowl had a chip in it.

I'd spent the last seven months collecting signs of danger, and that—that one little chip—was the clearest sign of all. It was so small, only about the size of my pinkie nail, but it seemed to explain everything.

• • •

I'd never been scared of blood. That wasn't some exaggeration or me trying to be tough, it was just the truth.

I'd gone off BMX ramps on Nate's bike and played street

hockey and wiped out on my board so much that my mom had started buying three of everything when she went shopping for my school clothes.

I'd watched boxing and WWF with my dad, and I'd seen football players destroy their knees on TV, and sometimes there were fights at school and someone got a bloody nose. The trashy boys or the rocker girls would flail around until the vice principal or the gym teacher waded into the crowd and pulled them apart, then told us all to go back to class. I watched horror movies—as many as I could—and never got tired of the bloody parts.

My dad understood me better than most people, and even he didn't really get what I liked about monsters. He was more into spy flicks, but he liked that I was interested in something he hadn't taught me.

His friend Ron had worked on a movie lot for a while and knew all the secrets to a really good splatter-fest. He told me they made the blood out of colored corn syrup and that was why it looked so fake onscreen. I nodded, but the truth was, even the football injuries and the school fights never seemed real. The blood always seemed a million miles away.

The first time I saw Neil beat Billy, it wasn't like any of those things.

The day I met him, Billy was already angry and out of control, but after they moved in with us, it got much worse. Or maybe he had always been like that, and now I was just close enough to see it.

He had been driving around Mission Valley and had gotten pulled over. When Neil found out, he became very quiet, and his eyes went cool and steady in the way I'd learned to be nervous about.

I was sitting at the kitchen table with a bent paper clip and a bottle of nail polish remover, cleaning the bearings on my skateboard, while my mom leaned on her elbows at the counter, flipping through a home decorating magazine.

Billy was standing at the open refrigerator, drinking out of the milk carton because my mom hated when he did that, and when Neil came in, holding the ticket like a flag, we all looked up. "This is how you spend your time? On this reckless, irresponsible nonsense?" Then he crumpled it up and threw it at Billy.

Billy turned to face him, letting the refrigerator door swing shut.

I stared hard at the label on the nail polish remover.

Since that day in the garage with the cigarette, things had been tense. Billy had always been rude and nasty to my mom, and it had been worse since the Hargroves moved in. He got mouthy with her when he thought he could get away with it, but I'd never seen him talk back to his dad. And in this moment he didn't say anything.

When Neil hit him, I didn't understand what had happened at first. It looked like something in slow motion.

For a second, we all just froze, like no one knew what was supposed to come next.

I looked over at my mom, sure that she'd be horrified, and needing her to fix it the way she had that day in the garage. The scene was bad, but it would all be okay, because she'd go to Neil and use her sweet, let's-all-get-along voice and make it stop.

But she didn't. She was standing at the counter, staring down at her magazine, her hair falling in a brick-red curtain over her forehead, hiding her expression. What was happening on the other side of the kitchen was bad enough, but the way she stood there looking at her hands, it was almost like she expected it.

When Neil hit him, Billy stumbled, but he didn't back away. Neil wound up to hit him again, and my mom still didn't say anything or try to stop it. This time, Billy fell back against the little wall shelf where my mom kept her recipe box and her painted teacups. The forget-me-not blue one smashed on the floor, and she didn't even look up.

Suddenly I understood in the worst, clearest way that this wasn't a surprise. Or at least, it wasn't so much of a surprise that she would leave. The idea that you could see someone hit his son like that and still pick him was terrible. My dad was forgetful and a slacker and kind of shady, but at least he never acted like a psycho. He never hit anyone. And still she'd left him and saddled us with whatever angry, twisted thing Neil was offering. She'd *picked* this for us.

Billy was trying to stand, slow and unsteady. He got his legs under him, but he was still bent over, with one hand on the floor and his feet apart, like he was trying to keep his balance in an earthquake. There was blood on his bottom lip, a little, and a puffy half-moon around his eye.

"You are going to learn respect," Neil said, moving to stand over him. "Respect, and responsibility."

My mom got up and went into the other room. She did it in a vague, vacant way, like she'd just remembered there were cookies in the oven and she needed to take them out.

With one hand, Neil undid the buckle on his belt, and for a second, I didn't understand. He was standing over Billy, staring down at Billy's bent back as he yanked his belt out of the loops. The way his eyes slid out of focus, it was like he wasn't even seeing Billy anymore.

I could almost forgive my mom for leaving. I'd never been squeamish about anything, and still I had an urge to look away. I was so wildly sure I wasn't supposed to see this, I wasn't supposed to be here. I still half believed that any second he'd glance around and remember I was there, and it would all stop. He'd see me sitting at the table with my paper clip still in my hand and that would be enough to make him catch himself and put down the belt. He just needed to remember I was there.

But Neil didn't even glance at me. He stood over Billy, folding the belt in half, doubling it over in his hand. I held my breath and waited.

The sound it made was thick and ugly. I felt it in my teeth.

Billy hunched his shoulders, but he didn't yell or try to duck away, and that was worse. I knew, in a deep, unhappy way, that this was wrong, I just didn't know how to stop it. I'd always known my mom was timid and kind of a pushover. I hadn't really believed she would let something get this bad, though. I'd never thought that she was weak before.

I wondered for the first time if things could be too scary for grown-ups to deal with. My mom was gentle and soft. She always complained that I was too callous and too much like my dad—that he had me in his pocket. But that was nothing compared to her. Neil had her in his fist.

Neil let the belt dangle, swinging it in a loose, lazy way, like he was winding up. I set my teeth and winced, imagining what it would sound like when it landed.

Billy watched the end of it with a resigned look, like a dog I saw in the back of the animal control van once, staring out of the wire mesh with this helpless mix of fear and fury.

Neil planted his feet and raised the hand with the belt. "Are you ready to take your punishment?"

"Stop it!" I shouted it. I hadn't known I was going to say anything until it came tearing out of me. It felt jagged, like I'd been holding something inside.

Neil turned, and for a second, looking into his eyes was like looking right into the sun, blank and dazzling. Then he smiled a tight, mechanical smile and turned back to Billy. "Is this the son I raised? A worthless loser who needs a little girl to fight his battles for him?"

He said it with so much wonder and disgust that I felt my face get hot and my eyes fill up.

In that second, I believed it—that he was right, that I was no one, just a little girl and there was no way to stop someone like him. He was a grown-up.

Neil set his jaw and swung the belt. He did it without hurrying, like it wasn't a big deal. He did it the way Mrs. Haskell down the street beat the dust out of her rugs. When he was done, he didn't look at either of us or say anything else. He just turned and walked out of the kitchen.

I sat with my hands clasped, fingers locked together like we were about to say grace.

Billy was still on the floor. He was on his hands and knees under the shelf where my mom kept her teacups. The blue one was in pieces around him. It looked like a broken Easter egg.

When the silence had lasted too long to deal with, and I was sure Neil was gone, I pushed my chair back and got down next to Billy. I knelt on the floor, sweeping the broken cup out of the way. Some of the fragments stuck to my hand, and I brushed them off on my pants. "Are you okay?"

It was such a stupid question. Billy was kneeling on the linoleum with his head down. He was so very far from okay. I thought he'd ignore me, or maybe tell me what a moron I was. Instead, he just stayed like that, staring at the floor. "Get away from me, Max."

The place around his eye was puffing shut, and I leaned to get a closer look. The skin was turning from beet-red to purple. If he put a frozen TV dinner on it, maybe that would take the swelling down.

I knelt there, remembering what he'd said to me in the parking lot of Captain Spaulding's and the nervous, hopeful feeling I'd had then, like we were in some sort of secret club together—like we could be on the same team.

"Do you want me to get you some ice?"

He looked up then, and I could see all the ways he hated me. His mouth twisted, and he turned on me like a snapping dog. "I *said,* get away from me."

The sound of his voice was the sound of an animal, horrible and savage. This time, I did what he said.

CHAPTER ELEVEN

Already, Hawkins was starting to feel small, like I was bumping around inside a fishbowl. Every day, I saw the same faces, walked into the same classrooms, waited for the bell, and then walked out again. I passed the same people in the same little cliques of threes and fours, and they always glanced at me, stared a beat too long, then looked away again.

I tried hard not to be mopey or think about the A/V boys anymore. It had been fun while it lasted, but they'd made it clear I didn't belong with them. No matter how much I wanted the company or how hard I tried to earn it, they didn't want me around. And as terrible as that felt— being shut out by the only people who'd been even a little bit friendly to me—I had to remember it was better that way. Being on my own was nothing compared to what Billy would do if he found out that I'd made friends.

Saturday was usually my favorite day, but with nowhere to go and no one to hang out with, what was the point? I tried to think of something to do, but everything felt like one big letdown. I could skate around the shabby downtown again, or else spend an hour or two alone at the arcade. Video games seemed a little lonely now, but at least it would pass the time. I was ready to burn through some quarters and forget about my real life for a while.

• • •

The Palace Arcade was full of loud, sweaty high school boys, and the carpet was crunchy and smelled like nachos. Still, blowing up a few monsters would make the day go faster. When I came up to the *Dig Dug* cabinet, though, I stopped short. There was an OUT OF ORDER sign taped to the screen.

I stood in the aisle between rows of games, looking at it. This was it, the story of my life. One more thing that had been nice while it lasted.

I was about to go look for a *Galaga* or a *Pac-Man* instead, or maybe just turn and walk out altogether, when the tall, oafy guy who ran the counter came over to me. He was always working when I came in, and didn't seem particularly friendly, but he'd obviously noticed that this was my game.

He was eating Cheetos out of the bag and looking how he always did—inscrutable. "Sorry about that, Road Warrior."

I must have seemed pretty desperate, because he shoved another Cheeto into his mouth and said, "Fret not. I got another machine up and running in the back."

The back office was basically just a storage room. I stood and waited while he unlocked the door. When he pushed it open, though, I saw that I'd been set up. This was a mom-and-pop arcade in a tiny town in Indiana: there was no backup *Dig Dug*.

Instead, Lucas was waiting for me, fiddling around with a broken *Asteroids Deluxe* machine.

The manager waved me inside and nodded to Lucas. "Keep things PG in here." Then he winked and left me there, feeling totally stupid.

I was supposed to have known better. After all, I'd encountered a whole parade of untrustworthy guys, able to trick my mom in a thousand ways. It was new, and unsettling, being the one who fell for things.

Lucas's face was open and anxious, if totally sincere, and I wanted to know exactly what was so important that he was ready to fake a broken game just to talk to me.

I marched into the office and sat down. He was perched on a stack of boxes, looking so serious I was a little worried.

The story was a real whopper.

According to Lucas, back when Will had disappeared, he wasn't actually lost. Or at least, he wasn't lost in the woods in some basic, normal way. He'd been gone, all right, but he was someplace else. At first, I didn't get what Lucas meant, but then I started to understand that he was talking about another *place,* not like lost in the city or the airport, but . . . lost. Somewhere no one had ever heard of or knew how to get to.

I just looked at him, shaking my head. When he'd told me the story before, I'd been skeptical, but whatever. It wasn't totally out of the question that someone could disappear. I was a whole lot less convinced that someone could disappear into an undiscovered world, and as Lucas talked, I got madder. My face felt flushed and prickly.

The story got more and more outlandish from there. The place where Will had gotten lost was not just any old world, but a world full of monsters. Not only *that*—Dart was one of them.

Yes, Dustin had found a baby monster and taken it to school in a homemade ghost trap, and then waited around to see what would happen, while it just kept getting bigger, but somehow it was my fault because I'd let it escape.

The whole thing was so ridiculous that I wanted to laugh. I wanted to shove him backward off his seat for telling me such an insane story.

But it didn't even end there! No matter how ridiculous I thought the story had gotten, Lucas was ready to one-up himself. They couldn't let me in the club because there was some huge government conspiracy and there was a special program, and men from a secret lab who would come after us if they knew we knew, and this whole alternate plane of existence full of monsters and we would all be in deep trouble if anyone found out we knew. There was a creature called a Demogorgon. There was a girl with magical powers who fought it and saved the town, maybe the world, then disappeared back through a hole in the wall, and no one had seen her since.

When he said that part, I thought I understood. The girl in the story was the same one Mike had talked about in the gym—El, the Mage.

It all sounded so fake, like a comic book or a make-believe game they were playing.

It was one thing to leave me out, have their secret meetings in the A/V room, and go on their stupid fantasy adventures without me. But it was another thing to try to trick me just to have something to laugh about. And if they were so determined to make me feel like an idiot, maybe they should have picked a better story instead of this wild, impossible fantasy that no one with half a brain would ever believe.

My dad didn't lie to me, but he had no problem lying to other people, and he was usually smiling when he did it. I'd gotten good at spotting liars. But Lucas wasn't even trying to seem slick. His eyes were wide and plaintive, like he was begging me to believe him.

When he was finally done with the story, I leaned back in my chair, keeping my face cool and amused. It seemed better not to care. I was sure it was all some big joke and it seemed very important, suddenly, to show how seriously I wasn't taking him. It was better than letting him see how mad it made me to have him treat me like an idiot. Like I was that gullible.

As soon as I stalked out of the office, he followed me, still spouting his elaborate story. But I was done listening.

Out in the arcade, I stopped and faced him. "You did a good job, okay? You can go tell the others I believed your lies."

As I turned to go, he caught me by the arm. "We have a lot of rules in our party, but the most important is, friends don't lie. Never ever. No matter what."

"Is that right?" I peeled the OUT OF ORDER sign off *Dig Dug* and waved it at him. Whatever noble rules they lived by in their little club, it had nothing to do with me. I wasn't part of their party. They'd made that abundantly clear.

He sighed. "I had to do that. To protect you."

That was it. I couldn't keep my voice low anymore, and I started to list all the random stuff he'd told me about the government and the monster and the girl.

Lucas lunged forward and covered my mouth with his hand. "Stop talking. You're going to get us killed." His face was earnest and unhappy, and in that second, I stopped being thoroughly convinced that he was laughing at me and started to think maybe he believed it.

"Prove it."

"I can't."

"What, so I'm supposed to just trust you?"

"Yes."

Suddenly I froze. The rumble of the Camaro echoed from the arcade parking lot.

I'd gotten used to listening for it. Back home, it had been the sound that meant the fun was over. I'd be hanging out at the rec center for drop-in floor hockey after school, or at the roller rink for teen-skate, and the Camaro would start revving up outside, and I'd know it was time for me to go.

Before I had time to think, I reached over and clutched Lucas's hand. "Don't follow me out." His hand was warm in mine, but all I could think about was what Billy would say—what he would do—if I came out to the car and he saw Lucas.

I dropped Lucas's hand and he opened his mouth to say something else, but I didn't wait.

Outside, the Camaro was idling in the parking lot. I climbed into the passenger seat, trying to seem like everything was normal. The engine ran rough in the cold, and the heater was blasting against my face. Even the rush of hot, dry air smelled like cigarettes.

Billy was looking past me. "What did I tell you?"

At first I didn't understand. Then I glanced toward the door and saw Lucas retreating back into the arcade. When I checked Billy's face, I understood with a sinking feeling that things were about to get bad. Lucas must have come and stood in the doorway, and Billy must have seen.

I'd been so careful not to let Lucas follow me. Unbelievable. This whole time, he'd been practically begging me to listen to his story, but he hadn't trusted me enough to stay inside, where Billy couldn't see him.

Thinking that made me feel like a hypocrite, though. I hadn't told him why he needed to stay.

I was talking way too fast, trying to convince Billy that there was nothing going on. And there wasn't, not really.

"Well, you know what happens when you lie." He said it in a light, matter-of-fact way that still sent an arrow of fear through my chest. His voice was brutal underneath.

I did know.

We drove in silence. Billy was drumming along to Metallica, his cupped hand thumping on the steering wheel.

I was still thinking about Lucas. His story was impossible. Not just wild, but actually impossible. There were no monsters. At least, not the kind he was talking about.

Billy was the closest thing to one that I had ever known. If Lucas wasn't careful, he was going to get hurt, and I wouldn't be able to do anything about it.

I told myself that it wasn't my fault. That this was what it meant to live with the monster standing right behind you. Even though it's yours—you're the one it's after, the one standing in its shadow—it will still take a wide, nasty swipe at anyone who gets close enough.

The Halloween movies understood that; the message was very clear. Even in the sequels, Michael Myers is just stalking his way through Haddonfield, on a mission to find his baby sister, and when he does, he's going to kill her. That's it, his whole plan. His obsession. He wants to kill her so bad that he broke out of an institution to find her. The thing is, he's a merciless killing machine. He might have an end goal, but he's not particular about how he gets there. And along the way? It's everyone else who dies.

• • •

The day everything changed, Nate and I were hanging out in the ditch behind my house.

We'd been working on our bike ramp all week, building it out of plywood and scrap lumber down in the bottom of the creek bed. When it was done, it was going to be the biggest one we'd ever built. Ben had brought some leftover house paint for the supports, and Eddie brought a posthole digger from his mom's garden shed that we'd used to sink the supports deep in the crumbly dirt so the ramp wouldn't wobble when we hit it.

The ground where the dead cat had been was still burned black at the top of the ditch, but the bushes were already turning green again, and the weeds were starting to grow back.

It had been overcast since noon, but the afternoon was hot, and the hill buzzed with the sound of grasshoppers and cicadas whirring in the grass.

Nate was sitting up at the top of the ditch with his notebook, drawing out plans, figuring out the angles for the struts. We had some framing nails and Nate's dad's toolbox and a pile of scrap wood we'd bought for seven dollars at the hardware store.

I was hot and sticky, and the palms of my hands were raw and sweaty from the rubber grips of the posthole digger, but I worked anyway, sinking the supports and patting the dirt down around them. We had picked the widest, deepest part of the ditch to build our ramp. When it was finished, it was going to be big enough to launch us into space.

"Where's the hammer?" I asked, lining up a pair of boards and trying to hold them steady with one hand while I felt around in the pile of tools with the other.

Nate made a note in his book and didn't look up. "Under the plywood, I think."

I found the hammer and retrieved it from the pile of loose boards lying in the dirt around the tool belt.

The air in the bottom of the ditch was still and quiet. There weren't even any mosquitoes. I was glad that today it was just the two of us, but it felt a little strange, a little off. "Where are Ben and Eddie?"

Ben and Eddie had been pulling weeds for Mrs. Harris in the mornings, but they usually showed up at my house by two or three. We hung out together almost every day, and for the last three years, they'd spent almost as much time in the bottom of the dry creek as Nate and me. But in the last week or two, they'd been around less and less. It wasn't like they'd been avoiding me, exactly, because we were still friends. I'd just seen them at the pool on Friday and we'd taken turns cannonballing off the diving board, but they'd pretty much stopped coming over, and I was starting to wonder if maybe they just weren't interested in building ramps and waterballoon launchers anymore.

"Are they too cool for me or something?"

That made Nate stop writing and look up from the book. His forehead wrinkled, and he frowned. "No, not like that. They just had other stuff to do, I guess."

"Better than this?"

He shrugged but didn't say anything.

I gave him a hard stare. "What?"

He just ducked his head and wouldn't look at me.

"What?"

"They're not mad at you or anything. They just don't want to hang around your brother."

I narrowed my eyes and didn't answer. Billy was a constant part of my life, but he wasn't my brother. At first he'd been my idol and then, almost as fast, my new problem. And in the months since the wedding, he'd been turning into something even sharper and more jagged.

Nate kept his head down, looking like he wanted to apologize. "Don't get pissed off at them. They know it's not your fault."

"I'm not pissed off. They can just go build their own ramp if they want, and good luck finding someplace with a slope this good."

But I couldn't help feeling like it kind of was my fault.

For the rest of the afternoon, we worked on the ramp,

digging postholes for the struts and nailing boards into X's for the supports. We didn't talk about Billy, or the new weirdness with Ben and Eddie. If we had, maybe the day would have turned out differently.

We had just finished anchoring the supports when Billy and Wayne showed up.

They came crunching down into the creek bed in their motorcycle boots. They looked overheated and bleary-eyed. Billy's hair was artfully messy, curling over his forehead, and I knew he'd sprayed it that way on purpose. Wayne was wearing a red flannel shirt with the sleeves cut off. They looked weirdly lopsided together, like a car with a missing wheel. My friends weren't the only ones MIA. I hadn't seen Sid since the afternoon of the dead cat and the fire.

Billy and Wayne ambled over to the couch and sat down to watch us. The couch was still in its spot at the top of the ditch. It had been sitting there all summer, and the upholstery was getting pretty ratty.

Nate stayed sitting in the dirt with his legs crossed and his head down, trying really hard to pretend they weren't there. I straightened up and glared at them. "Go away. This isn't your creek, so go hang around somewhere else."

Wayne looked at me wide-eyed, then laughed in a high, jittering whinny that made my skin crawl. "Max is playing doctor with her boyfriend and doesn't want us to watch."

I refused to acknowledge his comment. Nate and I had never once done anything like that, but I could feel myself blushing anyway.

Even back before school let out, things had been getting that way. Everyone was starting to pair off. It was beginning to seem like the only thing anyone talked about was who was going out with who, who'd done under-the-shirt stuff and gotten to what base, and who was starting to get bigger up top. While I wasn't paying attention, it had gotten so that if you were a girl who hung out with boys just because you wanted to, no one believed you. It always had to mean you were someone's girlfriend.

Billy was watching me in a strange, thoughtful way. He leaned back and kicked his boots up on the milk crate, giving me a chilly look. "Is that true, Max?"

Over by the pile of scrap boards, Nate was still sitting in the dirt and staring at his notebook, but I could tell that he was listening. It made me furious that even up here in the ditch, Billy could just show up and mess around with my life. He was ruining everything.

He began to tap down his cigarettes, drumming the pack on his knee and staring at me. "I said, is that true?"

I picked up another nail and tightened my grip on the Craftsman hammer. "No."

"Then you need to be more careful who you hang out with. Unless you want people to think you're easy."

I raised the hammer and held the nail in place, but I was too mad to aim straight. The hammer came down at a bad angle and glanced off the tips of my fingers. I swore and hopped in a circle while Billy laughed.

I wanted to rearrange his face with the hammer. It wasn't

enough that he'd moved in and set up camp inside my life. In less than six weeks, he'd chased away Ben and Eddie. He'd taken over my spot behind the house. And now he was going to take Nate away too. He had to ruin anything I liked.

I wanted to act cool and over it, but my face was burning. "You just think that because the only time you hang out with girls is if you know they'll screw you."

As soon as I said it, I knew it was a bad idea. The way he looked at me was dangerous, and I understood that whatever happened next was going to hurt. He stood up. He looked very tall standing in front of the ratty old couch at the top of the creek bank. Then he was down in the creek bed with me so fast I flinched, so close I could feel his breath on my forehead. His boots were almost touching the toes of my Vans. "You need to worry a little more about what people think of you."

I clenched my jaw and tightened my grip on the hammer.

Billy's gaze flicked to my hand. I thought he'd be furious, but instead he laughed. "What are you going to do with that hammer, Max?"

I didn't answer.

Above us, in the shade of the sweet pea bush, Wayne was still sitting on the couch. Billy stood over me, smiling, his eyes never leaving the hammer. I thought he was going to grab it out of my hand, but he only leaned closer, his voice sly and wheedling: "What are you going to do, Max? Are you going to take a swing at me?"

I stuck out my chin and shrugged. "Thinking about it."

Nate put down his notebook and stood up. "Come on, Max. Let's go down to the park or something. We can work on the ramp another time."

I shook my head. "This is my spot and my ramp, and I'm not going to sit around the picnic shelter and do nothing just because Billy's a jerk. It was mine first."

I was talking to Nate, but I was still looking at Billy, so I saw when his face changed. In a second, he'd gone from bored and kind of amused to dangerous.

He shook his head sadly and smiled a wide, fake smile, but his eyes didn't change. "Ma-ax, don't be selfish, now. You gotta learn to share. We're *family*."

The word was a loaded one, sweet and sick like poison.

I didn't answer, just squared my shoulders and glared at him, still holding the hammer. I was clenching my teeth, blazing and furious, but I didn't know what to do. I wanted to be able to use a smirk or a stare or a single word the way he did, filling up space as some kind of weapon.

Billy gazed down at me, smiling, always smiling, and I stared back at him.

Nate had crossed the packed dirt. He stepped closer, and this time, he sounded angry. "Leave her alone!"

It took a lot to make Nate mad. He usually kept his mouth shut and put his head down until it was safe to come out again. When he did get mad, it was righteous.

The way he cared about what was right and fair reminded me of the Man-Thing. Nate was short and shy and skinny, and the dry creek bed wasn't anything like a murky swamp in the Everglades, but the way he was glaring at Billy with his head down had the same unarticulated fury. For the first time in a long time, I thought about motorcycle gangs and real estate developers and the Slaughter Room. The way the Man-Thing had vanquished all of them. I was glad someone would defend me, even though I knew deep down there was nothing Nate could do.

Wayne was still hunched on the couch, watching and laughing his crazy laugh. It was higher now, and nervous.

Billy didn't laugh. He grabbed Nate by the elbow and shoved his arm behind his back. At first Nate didn't struggle or make a sound, and then he did. His eyes watered, and he gave a short, sharp cry. His face was going red.

Billy shoved harder, and Nate pressed his lips together, closing his eyes. Wayne had stopped laughing and gotten to his feet. Now he just looked sick and helpless, standing there in the weeds.

"Stop it, Billy!" I said it in a hard, flat voice, already sure this wasn't happening, so horribly sure that it wouldn't turn really ugly, because it couldn't.

Billy grinned, forcing Nate's arm up so high his hand was jammed between his shoulder blades. "Stop it? Stop what, Max? Stop this?"

Afterward, all I could think about was how his voice had sounded so bright and cheerful. It didn't match what was happening on his face. His eyes were full of a terrible nothing—chilly and faraway.

The sound was loud. It was like water poured over ice, or the sudden crack when a rock hits a windshield. Then Nate gave a howl and collapsed on his knees in the bottom of the creek bed, holding his arm awkwardly at his side. Billy stepped back, and at first I didn't understand. I thought that would be the end of it—it was obnoxious and ugly, but it was over. And then I saw the reason Nate's knees had given out. His elbow was bent the wrong way. His face went white in a way I didn't know happened in real life, like all the blood had dropped right out of him. We could see the pale knob of the bone jutting underneath his skin.

For a long time, none of us moved. Then Wayne turned away and struggled up out of the ditch. His boots sent a rain of dirt and gravel sliding down the bank to land in a little drift at my feet. He started in the direction of the street with his head down and without looking back.

Billy was still watching me in that strange, avid way that always made me feel like I was being x-rayed. His face was blank, but his eyes were full of a bright, glittering light, the way Mrs. Haskell's German shepherd Otto got when he was looking at a cat.

Billy breathed in through his nose and leaned closer. "What are you going to do, Max?"

I didn't say anything. Nate was slumped forward with his head bent, making a low wheezing noise, but I didn't go to him. I was suddenly sure that showing any kind of tenderness in front of Billy would make it worse. I'd seen what had happened to Billy when I tried to help him. Neil had mocked him for it, and that was bad enough. But Billy had *hated* me. I wanted to be a good friend, but I couldn't do the right thing, the brave thing, not even to help Nate.

Billy was standing over me, blocking my way. "You're going to be a good little girl and keep your mouth shut. Right?"

Behind him, Nate was crying now in soft, hitching gasps, holding his arm against his chest.

Billy leaned very close to my ear and said it again: "Right, Max?"

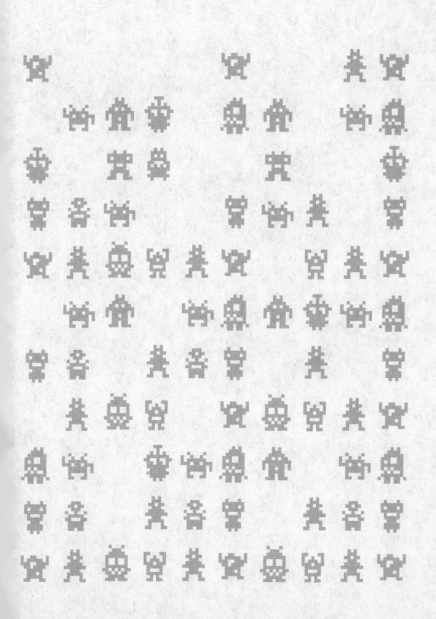

CHAPTER TWELVE

He said it was an accident. That's what he told his dad and my mom and the paramedics when we all stood out in the driveway after the ambulance came.

He'd been showing Nate a Hulk Hogan wrestling move and his hand had slipped, was all.

His smile when he said it was weird and empty, and I was so sure there was no way the grown-ups would be able to look at him and think he was telling the truth. I hadn't accounted for how hard they wanted to believe he wasn't a psycho. I was tempted to give up and tell them everything, but there was no guarantee the truth would make a difference. Nothing would magically fix Nate's arm. It seemed better just to nod along.

Even Nate didn't argue. He sat stone-faced on the stretcher and didn't say anything, even when they braced his arm with bandages and padded boards and loaded him in the back of the ambulance.

I called him when he got home from the hospital. I wanted to say that I was sorry, but the words wouldn't come out right. I sounded careless and too bright, like nothing mattered.

"My place was crazy after you left," I said. "But it's mostly cooled down. I just didn't think he would actually do that, you know?"

Nate should have shouted at me, or at least told me to stop acting so normal. Instead, all he said was, "I know."

After that, though, he didn't come over to work on the ramp anymore. The frame sat half-built, boards bleaching in the sun. After a while, when I finally accepted that none of them were coming back, I finished it by myself. My dad had taught me how to cut mitered corners and I was good with the handsaw and the level, but I was still just one person, and the sheets of plywood were heavy. It took me four days.

School in San Diego started two weeks later, and I went back not knowing if I had friends at all anymore. On the first day, there was Nate, sitting over at the group table on the other side of the room, with his arm in a cast. At lunch, everyone crowded around to sign it—even Mrs. Mallard the

French teacher, who hated me, and kids who never used to talk to us. I felt too awkward to sign it myself, and he didn't ask me to.

It was better that way. At least, that's what I was starting to believe. I had a bad feeling that putting my name on it wouldn't be a friendly gesture, but more like I was admitting to something.

Nate still picked me first for dodgeball sometimes, and when I got in the cafeteria line behind him or sat next to him in shop class, he didn't tell me I couldn't, but his eyes were always looking past me now.

Billy was dangerous, and he would keep getting more dangerous until someone got hurt. I could do my best to try to keep him happy, but not forever. Maybe not even for long. There was a time when I'd actually believed I knew how to handle him. I wouldn't make that mistake again. The whole point of movies was that monsters could be beaten. The point of the sequels was that they always got back up.

I knew what Billy had done to Nate was no accident, but I didn't know how to stop it.

Billy's rages were like the storms that blew in sometimes during fall. They happened suddenly, after days of clear blue sky. It would have been easy to say that he'd learned the trick from Neil, but Neil always wanted you to think that everything he did was so reasonable. He got satisfaction out of being the one who always seemed in control. Billy liked chaos better.

After Nate, I thought for sure that Billy had really messed up. He'd get sent to military school or wind up in jail or something. He was out of control in a way I didn't know how to deal with, and finally everyone else would see it too. But Neil and my mom wouldn't even say out loud what he'd done. They acted like they didn't get it.

Even later, when they'd already decided we were moving to Indiana, they never talked about the real reason, and when I tried to get them to say it, they gave me made-up ones instead. It would be good for us. It would give Billy a fresh start, away from his trashy, friends and other bad influences. It would give me a place to run and jump and play, with clean air and wide streets and less traffic.

They acted like it was this favor they were doing for us. Like Billy wasn't the ringleader of every kind of trouble he and his scuzzy loser friends got into, and I was six instead of thirteen. They still wouldn't admit the real reason: Billy was completely out of control and we were skipping town and hoping things didn't get worse.

I'd been an idiot before, when I'd believed in family and security. I knew the truth now: The world is a big, chaotic place, and you're totally on your own. You might as well keep your monsters close. That way, they never take you by surprise.

The night everything actually changed and we found out we were moving, I'd just gotten home from playing *Pac-Man* at Joy Town.

Neil was standing on a chair in the living room, taking down the row of framed travel postcards my mom had hung over the back of the couch.

For a minute, I stood and watched him lift each one off its hook and set it in the growing stack on the coffee table, but I didn't think it meant anything big. Of course he was taking them down. This was Neil, who didn't like any lamp or clock he hadn't picked out himself. He'd already reupholstered the old footstool and gotten rid of the rug in the hall, and now he was just ruining one more part of my old, familiar life. After all, he'd already ruined everything else.

"What are you doing with those?" I said, half thinking that maybe if I didn't seem like I wanted them too much, he'd let me keep them in my room.

He glanced down at me, but instead of answering, he turned and called, "Billy, come on in here. Susan, you should be here for this too."

My mom came in from the kitchen and stood in the doorway. We all waited, not talking, until finally Billy came slouching in, looking bored. He dropped down next to me on the couch, and Neil got down from the chair.

He stretched and then dusted his hands on his pants, even though the postcard frames hadn't been dirty. "Susan," he said, but he was still looking at Billy. "Do you want to tell them?"

My mom smiled weakly. "We have some big news, you guys."

She was trying to sound cheerful, but her voice wobbled and then went up at the end, like she was asking a question. My first thought was that they were going to have a baby, and right away I started to factor in one more hostage to worry about. One more soft, fragile thing that would need to be kept safe from Billy.

After a second, though, I decided that wasn't it. My mom looked nervous, but not happy or excited. I waited.

"We're moving," she said. "The bank offered Neil a transfer. There's a branch in Indiana, and—"

The room was folding in, getting smaller and brighter and way too hot. She went on, talking in that same high, bright voice, like this was all part of some great adventure. But I didn't really hear anything after *Indiana*.

Billy stood up. His face was furious and hazardous. "This is such crap."

I put my hand on the arm of the couch, feeling how shabby and worn-out the upholstery was, how rough.

Neil turned to Billy, and his tone was icy. "You're going to want to take some time in your room to cool off."

The edge in his voice told me that, underneath his calm, reasonable mask, he was itching for a fight, and I waited for things to get worse. Billy just turned his back on Neil and stalked off down the hall. On his way, he cursed and slammed his fist against the wall. My school picture from fifth grade shuddered and fell. It wasn't the same as taking a swing at Neil, but it was close enough. I waited for Neil to react the way he always did, to blow past talking and go straight to discipline. To the belt. Instead, he just watched Billy go with that bland, bored look.

"There's a putty knife in the garage," he said, turning to me. "Run and get it, and I'll pop these picture hooks out of the drywall."

I didn't want to run and get anything for him, but I did it. My heart felt like it was too big for my rib cage and was crawling up into my throat. My face was tingling.

I was almost to the laundry room, passing the dark doorway to Billy's room, when he stepped out into the hall and reached for me.

I tried to twist away, but I wasn't fast enough. He caught me by the arm, and it wasn't the first time he'd ever touched me, but other times had always been to push me out of the way in the kitchen or flick the end of my nose. This time, his fingers closed hard around my elbow. I gasped.

He leaned down so his mouth was right next to my ear. "You did this."

I held very still. There was a smudge on the wall behind him, and I stared at it.

Billy's voice was so low it seemed like I was feeling it, not hearing it. His thumb was pressing into the crook of my elbow so hard my hand was starting to go numb. "Look at me."

When I still didn't look away from the smudge, he gave me a little shake, talking through his teeth, low and dangerous. "Look at me, Max."

This time, I did.

His face was close to mine. His breath was hot and metallic. I could smell stale cigarettes in his hair. "I'm going to destroy you for this."

His eyes were a dead, dull color I'd never seen before, like looking into a black hole. My mouth was very dry.

Maybe back at the start of it all, standing in front of the Skee-Ball stalls at Fort Fun, I would have thought he was joking. Even after he burned the dead cat, and gave me the cigarette just to annoy my mom. Even after all the times he'd done crazy, reckless things and the times Neil had punished him for it, I would have told myself that was just Billy. It was just a game. But now all I could see was the sick, busted angle of Nate's arm.

"I didn't do anything."

He leaned down so his forehead was almost touching mine. "You've got a big mouth, Max."

His voice was low and ominous. I could feel it in my teeth. I shook my head, fast and breathless. There was no version of things that wouldn't have ended with my mom calling the ambulance. It wasn't like we could have left Nate there. He couldn't have just gone home without anyone noticing. "What was I supposed to do?"

Billy gave me a long, level stare. Then he raised his chin and let me go. "You're lucky I'm around to watch out for you. Remember that."

He left me standing in the doorway to the laundry room. There was a hot, achy place on my arm, throbbing in time with my heartbeat. When I looked down, there was a red mark the size of his thumb.

"Maxine," Neil shouted. "Did you get lost in there?"

"No, sir," I called back.

After I'd brought Neil the putty knife, he got back up on the chair and pried the picture hangers out of the drywall. I went in my room and opened my dresser. Since the wedding, Neil and my mom had been getting kind of weird about letting me see my dad, and now they were going to take me away from him altogether—take me halfway across the country with Billy. I put some socks and underwear and two pairs of jeans in my backpack. The next night, I took a twenty-dollar bill out of my mom's jewelry box and did the only thing I could do.

I left.

• • •

At home, Billy pulled into the garage so he could change the Camaro's spark plugs with the door up and the music blasting. I stayed out in the driveway with my board.

I was practicing my kick flips, when my mom called to me from the screened-in porch. "Max, could you come and help me hang this picture?"

I sighed. "Can't it wait? I'm busy."

Neil was climbing the front steps, carrying a box of power tools. "Put down that skateboard and do what your mother tells you, Maxine."

I wanted to roll my eyes at him, but I dropped my board and went to help her with the picture.

We were just making sure it was straight, when out in the garage, we heard the music shut off and the Camaro rev up. A second later, there was a huge, brittle crunch, and I knew what it was even before I looked.

Billy had backed over my board.

I leapt down the front steps and raced to see, hoping I was wrong. But it was just the way it had sounded. He'd crushed the deck with his back tire and the nose had splintered off completely.

I stood over it, looking at the damage. This was my punishment. It had to be. The price for being seen with Lucas.

"You jerk." I said it in a flat, furious voice. My cheeks were prickling in a hot, humiliating way, like I was going to cry, and I bit the inside of my lip hard.

The look Billy gave me was bored and heavy-lidded. "What do you want me to say, Max? Maybe if you didn't leave your stuff everywhere, it wouldn't get broken."

"You jerk!" This time I yelled it, stomping hard on the concrete.

We were facing each other in the driveway, standing over my broken board and shouting at each other, when Neil came back outside. He stopped on the steps, looking back and forth between us. "What's going on out here?"

"He wrecked my board!"

Billy threw up his hands. "She left it in the driveway!"

Neil gave both of us a hard, level stare. Then he turned to Billy. "Looks like you'll be giving your sister rides from now on."

Like we hadn't already been stuck with each other all week. I didn't want to get in the car with Billy. I never wanted to see him again, but Neil was giving us both a dangerous look, and I didn't say anything. I picked up the pieces and went inside.

• • •

I was frightened now. Billy's moods were bad enough, but I didn't like the way he'd looked at Lucas. He'd broken the board just to show me that he could, and that meant he might be planning to break other things. I knew beyond a doubt that this was too dangerous and messy for me to handle on my own.

I needed a grown-up, someone to step in and take over the situation for me. But my mom would never be able to keep Billy in line even if she tried, and Neil's way would just make everything worse. I needed someplace far away, where things were easy and laid-back and I wouldn't have to think about it anymore.

I needed my dad.

The problem with that was, no way in hell would my mom and Neil willingly send me back to California. The only way to get there was to go on my own, and the fallout would be bad if I got caught. If they'd freaked out about me running away when we were back in San Diego, it was going to be ten times worse now. I tried to decide if I could leave without them knowing. If I was brave enough to take the Greyhound all the way to LA from Indiana.

I was pretty sure I could handle it, but the trip was going to be a lot longer than the one from San Diego, and I'd have to do it without my mom noticing I was gone before I'd even gotten out of town. And the biggest issue was how much it was going to cost.

I wished I were a grown-up. Every problem would be so much easier with a bank account and a job. But then, if I were a grown-up, none of this would even be an issue. Grown-ups didn't have to deal with friends who abandoned them or with dangerous stepbrothers. When things got out of control, they could just leave.

The solution to all my problems came sooner than I'd expected, though.

After dinner on Friday, my mom was in an exceptionally good mood. She was bent over the newspaper with a pen, circling things in the Sears ad.

"Honey," she said, glancing up from the housewares section. "Neil and I are going up to Terre Haute tomorrow to see about getting some things for the house."

Billy made a disgusted noise. "What a joke. Hawkins doesn't even have a Sears."

My mom was still bent over the newspaper, talking in a vague, dreamy voice, like she hadn't heard him. "There's supposed to be a new mall opening in town soon. Star Land?

Star Court? But that's months from now. We need some new sheets and towels, and a snow shovel before the weather gets bad."

The shopping list was so fantastically boring I couldn't tell if she was saying it to us or to herself. I was considering my options, trying to shake the nagging sense that this whole idea was insane. The feeling I got when I imagined leaving was like the feeling I got from standing on the end of the high dive. Pretty soon, there was going to be snow. I'd never really seen snow, except on TV. I told myself that it was no big deal, just a sprinkling of frozen water. An unflavored shave-ice. I tried not to think about how I'd be missing it.

My mom glanced up from the paper like she could see what I was thinking, and I half expected her to ask me if there was anything I needed to tell her. But she just smiled her small, nervous smile. "I was thinking if you wanted, we could take you shopping for some new clothes? I bet the girls dress differently here."

They did, but they dressed like choir directors, and I was not about to start showing up to school in beige turtlenecks and plaid skirts. I was already talking myself through what came next. Terre Haute was at least an hour away. The shopping trip would mean they'd be gone all afternoon and I'd be alone in the house.

Alone except for Billy.

I knew that telling her I didn't want to go to Terre Haute was going to hurt her feelings, but it was my best chance.

171

In a day or two, her feelings were going to be pretty hurt anyway.

"No thanks," I said, trying to sound casual, and not like I'd rather be dead than walking around in a matching blouse-and-sweater set.

She looked kind of shattered, but all she said was, "Okay, maybe some other time?"

Even now that I knew when my opening would be, there was still another layer to the problem. Bus tickets cost money, and I didn't have any. Or at least, not the kind that would get you more than a round of *Pac-Man* and a slice of pizza. My mom almost never let me buy anything without asking Neil first, but I had an idea and I'd have to try. There was no other way.

I found her in the utility room, folding laundry out of the basket on top of the washer. I picked up a sock and started poking around in the basket, looking for its matching one.

She smiled in a bright, distracted way. "How thoughtful of you!"

I fiddled with the sock and immediately felt guilty. I didn't usually help her with the laundry. I needed to talk to her when Neil wasn't around, though, and he never helped with the laundry.

We stood facing each other in front of the washing machine. She smelled powdery and sweet, like perfume and fabric softener, and for a second, I felt really bad about what I was going to do next.

"I have to ask you something, but it's private. You can't tell Neil."

She was watching me, wide-eyed, and I realized I was scaring her a little. "What is it, honey?"

I took a deep breath and tried not to look as guilty as I felt. "About the school clothes. I do kind of want to go shopping?"

She looked at me with something so earnest and open it made me shrivel inside. The expression on her face was hope. "Really?"

I nodded. "I just was wanting to go by myself. The eighth-grade girls here are all nuts for jelly bracelets and lace tops, and they have some really cool ones in the window at that Cozy Closet place. I was thinking I could go down there and pick one out. With my friends." I had to be careful not to push it too far. Hopefully she'd believe in a version of me who was into jelly bracelets and had friends. "And . . . I was wondering if maybe I could get some volumizing mousse too. They have it at the drugstore?"

By that point, she should have been deeply suspicious, but she was looking at me in this warm, open way, like this was all she ever wanted, her rambunctious daughter turning into one of the good girls, nice and sweet and normal.

Her beaming smile gave me a shaky feeling, like I was slipping out of focus. I wanted to make her happy, but none of the things that would make her happy were things I could be without lying. When my mom looked at me, she saw a problem that needed to be solved. She saw someone too prickly and rude to feel good around, and too much like my dad to really understand.

It wasn't until I was back in my room, the bills in my hand, that I had time to feel guilty. It was a lot of money for her to spend on me, even if I had been telling the truth, and the part where I wasn't going to use it for the lace top made me feel really bad. I didn't know what else to do, though.

Someone should have told her I was too much like my dad to trust. But Billy was spinning out again, and things would be so much worse if I stayed. I didn't have any other options.

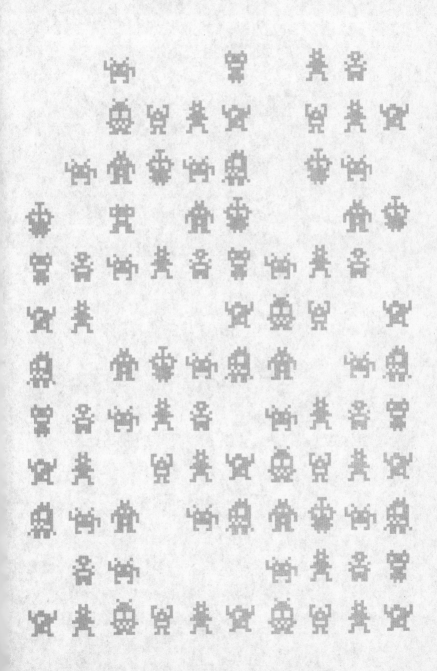

CHAPTER THIRTEEN

On Saturday, I got myself a box of Club crackers, two cans of Squirt, and my toothbrush and locked myself in my room. I packed the snacks in my backpack, along with socks, underwear, and an extra pullover. It wasn't much. I wished I had some Twinkies, but I'd have to live without.

My mom and Neil had left for Terre Haute that morning, and now I was just waiting for Billy to go out so that I could make a run for it.

He was camped out in the living room, lifting weights. The bench press was the same one he'd kept in the garage back home, but since the move, he'd been keeping it in the house. The garage here was cold and spidery and full of boxes.

He was doing curls with the barbell and drinking one of Neil's beers, with his music blasting and a cigarette jutting from his mouth. He'd always been intense about working out. Lately, though, whenever he was home, it was pretty much all he did.

I sat on the edge of my bed, trying to fix my skateboard deck and waiting for Billy to get tired of his workout routine. The backpack sat on the bed, packed with everything I planned to take with me. I'd have maybe three hours to get into town and find my way to the bus station. Then I'd figure out the schedule and catch the next bus for California.

At the very least I knew the ride would be long and boring. But it was hard to imagine the specifics. Once I got to LA, the rest of the trip was easier to picture. I'd find a pay phone and call my dad. He'd be confused at first, maybe even annoyed, but he'd understand. He wasn't supposed to have me full-time, but he was cool about stuff. If I explained the situation, he'd come and get me.

I pictured my new life in his apartment, sleeping on the pullout couch and eating cold takeout for breakfast. He'd stay up way too late calculating point spreads and working on weird inventions and spend all his nights and weekends at the bar or the track. But I could deal with that. I'd get used to it.

I stared at my backpack. Sneaking away meant taking barely anything with me, but I'd be fine without my stuff. I didn't need my comic books, or even most of my clothes. All I really cared about was my board, and it was in bad shape. Once I got to my dad's, maybe he'd be able to fix it.

My dad was good at the kinds of things they never taught us in school. My mom called him a jack-of-all-trades, but he actually only had three or four. When they were married, he used to hustle pool sometimes, and once he sold black-market tape decks out of the garage. Since the divorce, though, he'd gotten more careless. He'd keep a job for a couple months, usually as a repairman, or the cashier at a payday loan place, before he got fired. Or else got bored and quit. But his real job was getting people things they needed.

He could find old concert bootlegs or new license plates, if that was what someone was looking for. And he ran all kinds of betting, even the illegal kind.

He wasn't big on housekeeping or home decorating. His apartment was shabby and dark. But the kitchenette faced east, and he'd sit at the counter and drink his coffee in the mornings with the sun coming in through the shades in stripes, lighting him from behind. Sometimes if I was the first one up, I'd sit alone in the kitchen and picture how I must look, the sun coming through my hair like I was bursting into flames.

My favorite thing was watching him make fake IDs. He'd spend an evening sitting at the counter in his kitchenette, peeling the backings off old California driver's licenses, squinting down at the names and birth dates through a magnifying glass. There was something almost magical about watching him match the old pictures to new names, like watching people become someone else right in front of me.

He'd sit with his head bent and his fingers working to assemble the pieces, making new identities for people doing things he wouldn't tell me about. A lot of the jobs he did were things he wouldn't tell me about.

He didn't make the IDs very often. When he did, though, he would always let me watch.

I didn't know the exact word for what he was, but I knew enough not to tell my mom. He never said who they went to, just that he wasn't selling them to high school kids. I'd watched enough spy movies with him to know the score. A fake ID was for helping people disappear.

The last time I'd stayed with him, I'd stood at the counter in my stocking feet with a can of Coke and leaned next to him. He was gluing down a color photo the size of a stamp, setting it carefully in the corner of the ID with tweezers. The man in the photo was dark-eyed, with a stringy mustache. I knew him from the Black Door Lounge. He always came in to watch boxing on the weekends, and when I was younger he used to give me the cherries out of his old-fashioneds. His name was Walter Ross, and he hung out at the lounge with the rest of my dad's scuzzy friends. The ID was for someone named Clarence Masterson.

"That's Wally from the bar. Why does it say his name is Clarence?"

My dad smiled but didn't look up. "Because you need a really specific name to sell a new identity. Nothing sounds faker than *John Smith*. Two steps left, sweet pea. You're block-ing the light."

I moved out of the way, watching as he lined up the photo with a careful finger, then pressed it flat and held it there. I wondered where Wally was going and what he had done to make him want to be someone else.

Of course my dad would understand why I'd come. He was the kind of person who would get how it was to be in the place everyone said you should be and still just need to leave.

• • •

I was sitting on the edge of my bed, winding duct tape around the broken nose of my deck, when the doorbell rang.

Billy was out in the living room, ten feet from the door, but he didn't answer it and the bell rang again, an impatient double chime like someone was stabbing it with their finger. He dropped the weights and yelled for me to see who it was. I sighed and got up to go check, half-convinced it was just going to be some perky middle-aged lady going door-to-door selling Avon.

But I knew it wasn't. Ladies who sold Avon were uptight and fussy, even in Hawkins. They never really came out to Cherry Road.

When I opened the door, Lucas was standing on the steps, wearing a canvas jacket with a fake sheepskin lining and looking serious. My whole face felt cold.

I could see his bike behind him, keeled over on its kick-stand on the side of the road.

"I have proof," he said.

At first I wasn't totally sure what he was talking about. He was wearing a camo bandana tied across his forehead like Rambo, which didn't prove anything about anything, it was just weird.

I was a little freaked out by him showing up at my house. Any other time, I would have been happy to know that even after everything I said to him at the arcade, he still wanted to hang out with me. Now all I could think about was what was going to happen if Billy saw him. I didn't know how much time we had, but I needed him to leave.

Before Billy could turn around and see Lucas standing on the porch, I stepped outside and closed the door behind me. "Proof of what?"

He shook his head. "You have to come with me now."

It wasn't an answer to my question, because he *never* answered my questions, and I could feel myself starting to get angry again. "Where?"

Lucas pressed his lips together before answering. "You just have to trust me."

For a second, I stared at him. The longer we stood there, the more I started to think that we'd still be standing there when Billy came to see what was going on. The door would open, and he'd come up behind me, and then the scene would really get bad. "You have to leave."

Lucas was looking at me in that open, exasperated way

he had, where every particle of his attention was fixed on me, impatient, but completely, 100 percent honest.

"My window," I said finally. "Around back. It's the one with the firewood rack underneath. Meet me in thirty seconds."

I turned around and shut the door before Billy could come out and find Lucas there.

Billy was still in the living room, but he wasn't lifting weights anymore. When he reached for his beer and demanded to know who it was, I didn't let my face change. The way he was looking at me was sharp-eyed and too steady, like he knew something was up, he just didn't know what. Lucas had told me a story about monsters like he believed they were real, and I knew that it was true. Just not the way he meant.

After all, there was one in my house right now.

With my expression as blank as I could make it, I walked down the hall to my room and shut the door behind me. The backpack was sitting where I'd left it, waiting for me to scoop up my board and my jacket and make a break for it.

This was my shot, but suddenly getting back to my dad didn't seem like much of a solution to anything.

When Lucas came coasting around the side of the house on his bike, I was waiting at the windowsill. There was a part of me whispering that I was giving up what might be my best shot at California. I was going to miss my opportunity and regret it forever. But another, louder part of me insisted that Lucas was here for something important. If I didn't go with him now, I'd never have another chance.

I left the backpack sitting next to my broken skateboard.

Lucas had come all the way out to Cherry Road because he wanted to show me something, and whatever it was, I was pretty sure he believed it. I didn't really think it would be convincing—maybe not even any proof at all—but suddenly I needed to see it too.

I opened the window and climbed out.

CHAPTER FOURTEEN

Lucas rolled up on his bike, and I jumped down from the top of the wood box and got on.

He cut across weedy gravel driveways and through yards, staying off the road. I perched behind him on the back of the banana seat and held on to his shoulders. The afternoon was quiet and peaceful. It was gray and chilly out, and all the neighbors were inside. I should have been worried about where we were going or what kind of proof he meant, but the whole time I was listening for the Camaro.

I felt twitchy and breathless, expecting it to come roaring after us at any second. I knew that if Billy actually stopped working on his pecs for two seconds and noticed I was gone, he'd catch us in a heartbeat. He'd pull up next to us, give me that hard stare, and I'd have no choice but to get in. Everything else would fall away, and all I'd be able to see was the yawning mouth of the passenger seat.

But it wasn't just how easily I'd cave that made my throat hurt. I didn't know what he'd do if he found me with Lucas. Or, I knew, I just didn't know exactly how bad it would be, and that scared me worse than anything. The feeling it gave me wasn't like worrying about bus rides or disappointing my mom or whether I ever made friends again. It was a freezing, bottomless fear, and it covered everything.

Even without knowing the full situation, Lucas was careful not to go near the main road, though. We rode through the silent neighborhood, my hands on his shoulders. The canvas coat was rough under my fingers, and the shape of his shoulders was different from the bony, familiar way Nate's shoulders had felt. I could feel how the muscles in his back moved as he pedaled and how warm he was through his jacket.

We rode fast, not talking. I told myself that I'd only agreed to go with him in order to keep him away from Billy, but it wasn't quite true. That fear was being steadily overridden by another feeling, warm and glowing in my chest. He'd come to get me. And I was glad.

As Lucas put more distance between us and my house, I stopped worrying about Billy and started to be increasingly curious about where we were going. We weren't headed into town after all. Instead, we followed a weedy road up through a spindly stand of trees, and stopped at the top of a hill. We got off the bike, and Lucas took hold of the handlebars and walked it over to the other side of the slope.

We were looking down into a junkyard.

Lucas had a smug expression, and I was ready for him to explain why he'd brought me to the town dump. "What's going on? What are we doing here?"

Below us was a sea of rusty old cars with their taillights busted out and their doors torn off, mixed with ancient refrigerators and rusty sheets of corrugated metal. The whole place was a jackpot for building supplies.

Then I saw we weren't the only ones here.

At one end of the junkyard, Dustin was standing near a rickety old bus with an older guy, probably Billy's age. He looked irritated and kind of preppie, with a giant swoop of hair like someone in a new-wave band. They had a gas can with them and a baseball bat pounded full of nails, and weirdly, a bucket of meat. They were dropping the meat in a trail on the ground.

I turned to Lucas. "What are they doing down there?"

He jerked his head at Dustin and shrugged like it should be obvious. "Looking for Dart."

"In a junkyard? That doesn't—"

He held up a hand to cut me off. "I know, I know, that doesn't make sense. But you just have to trust me."

The whole thing was so supremely weird that I was tempted to stick around to see what happened next. I didn't really believe him, but I was kind of curious to see where this was going.

Lucas stashed his bike, and we headed down into the junkyard.

We cut a path through the weeds toward the bus. Everything about the scene was straight out of a horror movie, except that no one in horror movies wore Members Only jackets. I was pretty sure that the junkyard was abandoned—maybe out of commission five or ten years—and also that Lucas and Dustin had been here before.

"Steve," Dustin was saying as they stood in the center of the clearing. "Steve, listen to me. Dart has discerning tastes. It does *so* matter where we put the bait, and I'm telling you, this is the perfect spot."

The other guy just gave him a bored look and dumped out the rest of the meat in a pile.

The sun was setting, and I didn't know what I was doing there or when my mom and Neil would be getting back. I didn't have a coat, just my warm-up jacket, but I knew the icy, creeping feeling on my neck wasn't because of the dropping tempature. I was gripped by an eerie certainty that something was going to happen.

Lucas and Dustin had gone off to whisper about something—probably me—behind one of the dead cars, and I was left standing awkwardly in the clearing with Steve. I began to wonder where Mike and Will were, since Lucas hadn't mentioned anything about them and they were nowhere to be seen in the junkyard.

I waited for Steve to make some crack about my hair or my clothes, or act like a jerk the way high school boys always did, maybe even tell me to get lost, that this was private secret monster business.

But he just went over to one of the junk piles and started picking through it, pulling out sheets of scrap metal and lugging them across the clearing. I watched as he fitted pieces of battered plywood against the doors and windows. He was shoring up the bus.

After a minute, he turned and looked at me with one eyebrow raised. "Are you going to give me a hand, or what?"

I trotted after Steve, and together we started covering the smashed-out windows of the bus with mismatched sheets of plywood and scrap metal.

He held a square of aluminum siding in place and glanced over his shoulder. "So you're new in town?"

I nodded. It was the kind of question a retired neighbor or the lunch lady would ask you, weirdly adult, and I didn't know what else to do. Steve just nodded back and started pulling dented sheets of aluminum out of the drifts of junk and tossing them in a heap.

The whole afternoon had turned blurry and surreal, and everything about it was the strangest part.

Lucas and Dustin were still crouched behind the broken-down car, having some sort of very intense discussion that didn't include me. It was infuriating that no matter how hard I tried to understand their game, they would always be playing it without me.

Steve yelled for them to come help, and we worked in silence, dragging the scrap metal over to the bus and layering it to cover the windows.

The bus was a mess inside, the vinyl seats half-rotten and tilting on rusted legs.

Steve looked around like he was taking inventory. "We need to figure out some way to board up the windows and still be able to keep a lookout."

There was a hatch in the ceiling, square like a trapdoor. I glanced up. "If we can get on the roof, it'll be easy to see from there."

Steve looked down at me and raised his eyebrows. I thought he'd wave me off or say that it was a little kid's idea, but instead he nodded and clapped me on the arm. "Good thinking."

I hunted through the heaps of rusty buckets and warped boards until I found an aluminum ladder lying in the weeds. It was a little shaky, covered in tattered spider-webs and dry grass, but it seemed sturdy enough. I hauled it into the bus and leaned it so it jutted through the opening in the ceiling.

When I climbed up top, I could see all the way to the rooftops of the big Hawkins Lab compound—almost all the way to town. Another time, I would have gotten into the game. I would have felt excited about the whole after-noon, satisfied that we'd just built a pretty sweet fort. The more I watched the others, though, the more obvious it was that Lucas had been serious. None of them seemed very much like they were playing.

The roof of the bus was faded from the sun and speckled
th rust. From up here, you could see in every direction,
t it felt too exposed. Over in a weedy corner of the junk-
rd was a big pile of tires. I got back down and we searched
ough them, picking out the sturdiest ones, then rolling
m over to the bus one by one. The rubber was so old it
s cracking, and the tires left big smears of black stuff on
hands. We wrestled the tires up the ladder and stacked
m on the roof in an overlapping pattern to make a sort
ounker.

Steve was down in the center of the clearing, pouring
gas in a wide circle around the heap of meat. It was
mpletely weird to watch, but the meaning was obvious
ough: he was going to lure out whatever they were hunt-
and then set the trail of gas on fire.

The bus was rickety and rusted out, but after we were
ough, it was so heavily armored it looked like something
n *The Road Warrior.* With the reinforcements in place,
as straightened his bandana and climbed on top with
binoculars to keep watch. It had been a good call, bring-
the binoculars, but I had no idea what he was watching

teve and Dustin both followed Lucas into the bus, and
though neither of them bothered to explain what we
supposed to be doing, the meaning was clear: it was
to hunker down.

We sat and waited. The inside of the bus smelled like
s and mold. The amount of preparation we'd put in

seemed like overkill. Dart was about as big as a guinea [
the last time I'd seen him.

I tried my best to sit still and be patient, but I was getti
restless. The air was colder now and the sun had set co
pletely. Steve sat on the floor with his back against the bal
the bus, flicking the wheel on his lighter and then flipp
the top down to put out the flame.

Dustin was more animated. He fidgeted in the cram
little space behind the driver's seat, shifting from foot to f
and telling me all about the monster that had terrori
them last year and how Steve had fought it. The whole th
sounded ridiculous. Steve didn't exactly look like a hero,
a guy who'd spent all afternoon poking around the salv
yard with his collar popped and his sleeves pushed up.

"And you're, like, totally one hundred percent sur
wasn't a bear?" I knew I was pushing it, but it was still l
to believe this could be anything but a joke. No one c
out to an abandoned salvage yard to light a monster on
with a flip-top lighter and a can of gasoline and actu
meant it. That was kids' stuff. Fantasy.

Steve just nodded, leaning there with his lighter,
Dustin turned on me angrily. "What are you even d
here if you don't believe us? Go home!"

I knew he only meant it in a mean, petty way, lik
could punish me for daring to question the outrageous
ries they kept handing me. He didn't know the hardest
about going home was that I'd been trying to. The pro
was, no matter how much I wanted to be there, my

home might be too far to get to. For the first time, I let myself consider the possibility that it might not exist at all anymore, if it ever really had.

There was a blue-violet square of sky showing through the hatch in the roof, velvety and studded with tiny pin-prick stars. I climbed the ladder and clambered out onto the roof with Lucas. As we sat in the dark, waiting for whatever strange horror was coming, I still couldn't help thinking that this was all some giant practical joke. The small, sneaky voice in my head whispered that I was being tricked, but I had no idea how anymore.

The most obvious explanation for everything was that they actually believed it.

I still didn't know whether I did. Whether I *could*. The way I was going along with it didn't feel like belief, exactly, but still, the fact was I'd chosen this instead of a two-day bus ride. I'd chosen this over everything. It dawned on me that I would rather sit in a freezing-cold junkyard, waiting for some kind of monster to show up, than be safe in my living room with a plate of Oreos and a glass of Quik, watching *T. J. Hooker*. It was ridiculous, but it was true.

The roof of the bus was cold through my jeans. Lucas was crouched behind the wall of tires with his binoculars, scanning the junkyard.

A layer of fog had rolled in, thick and low to the ground. I watched it, remembering the smoke that had drifted around the men at the bar in the bus station. The creepy goblin story waiting to happen. Since morning, I'd been thinking more and more about that night in the bus station. I'd been so sure that I belonged there, hiding my face, running, that I'd been ready to do it again.

Now, when I really let myself imagine it, it scared me a little, how close I'd been to stepping right off the edge of my normal everyday life, with no net to catch me. How easy it had seemed.

I forced myself to actually imagine what it would be like once I was on the bus, probably sitting next to some sleazy burnout, and also once I got there, trying to find my way from the bus station all the way out to my dad's apartment in East Hollywood.

Even my dad was just playing a game, telling me about padlocks and secret messages because it was more exciting than the truth—that he was a small-time bookie with a bitter ex-wife and a daughter with an attitude.

That was what I'd been headed toward. A pullout couch in a cramped one-bedroom with dirty windows and a sticky floor. A small, grimy life in a place that barely even had room for my dad. And that was only if he didn't freak out and send me straight back here.

I still had a stubborn idea that he wouldn't do that, but it might have just been wishful thinking. I *wanted* to belong to him, but if I was being honest, I wasn't sure he had room for me. Not in the way I needed him to. Not every day. And when I was being *really* honest with myself, I admitted that I'd known that and had just been pretending.

I wondered how many people were playing a game

without really knowing that was what they were doing. For weeks I'd been telling myself that all I wanted was to go back to my dad, but when the chance came, at the last minute I'd picked the great unknown instead.

The fog didn't look so much like cigarette smoke in a bus station anymore. It looked like the ocean.

It was good to sit up here in the crisp, cold air with the stars spread out above us. I knew that no matter what, none of the people in my life were going to swoop in to help or make things better.

My mom tried, but she wanted me to be someone else. Billy was never going to fix anything. What he wanted for me was a fast, flashy world, bigger and more honest than my dad's, but violent and chaotic. The only things he liked about me were my worst parts.

Lucas was watching me, his eyes kind and expectant, like he was waiting for something. I wanted him to understand, but when I tried to say any of the hard parts out loud, I could only manage the simplest version. My eyes were blurry and wet suddenly, and I hated it. When I talked about my life, it felt like he was seeing too much of me. I didn't want him to think I was just some random girl who cried at stupid things.

He didn't act weirded out, though, or like crying made you weak.

He didn't say anything about it at all. "You're cool, Mad Max. I like talking to you."

The woods were full of noises—chirps and squeaks

and chittering—but they weren't the cries of birds, even whatever weird, unfamiliar birds lived in Indiana. We were sitting in the nest of tires, looking at each other, when there was a strange rustling below, and we both froze. Down in the junkyard by the edge of the clearing, something was moving.

At first, I didn't trust what I was seeing. The shape was dark against the pale backdrop of the fog. It had a sinewy body and a strange pointed head. It couldn't be Dart; there was no way. It had to be a trick of the light, and I was just seeing a dog or a coyote. A cougar, even. Not the hungry, angular thing that came slinking over the dry ground.

The monsters I understood were all just men underneath: Michael Myers, Jason, Leatherface. They loomed huge and hulking, hiding their faces behind masks, but they were still just flesh and blood.

The thing that had appeared down in the junkyard, slinking between the broken washing machines and dead cars, was not like anything I'd ever seen on TV or in the movies. All the monsters I had ever known were ordinary underneath. Even the mummies and vampires were actors in makeup when you looked close enough.

The meat was still lying in a gooshy heap in the clearing, surrounded by a circle of gasoline. The creature didn't come to it. When Steve opened the door to the bus and stepped out into the junkyard, I didn't understand what he was doing at first. Then I got it. He was using himself as bait.

He stood over the pile of meat, holding his spiked

oall bat and waiting for the thing to charge him. Instead
t stayed slow and low to the ground, like it was stalking

hat was when we saw the others. They slunk through
salvage yard from all sides. One had climbed up onto
of the rusted-out cars, and it was much closer. Dart; had
ght friends.

he junkyard echoed with clicks and trills, like the calls
reatures in a nightmare. And then we were screaming at
e, trying to get his attention, telling him to look. To run.
teve heard the urgency of our shouts and turned just
me. One of the dark, wiry shapes lunged, and he barely
out of its way, throwing himself across the hood of a
ed-out car. As soon as he hit the ground, he set his feet
swung like he was batting for the fences. The bat con-
ed with a *thunk,* and the creature fell back. So it might
been faceless and expressionless, but you could hurt it.
hen Steve was running, pelting back toward the bus,
the creatures scrambling after him. When they moved
the misty ground, I knew with horrible certainty that
s seeing something that did not belong in the natural
ld. Steve flung himself back inside, and Dustin slammed
folding door just in time.

Ve all flinched as the beasts threw themselves against
sides of the bus. I crouched between the seats, just try-
to feel like there was some kind of barrier between me
them. A fortress around me to protect me from the
sters. I'd seen them, I'd heard their high, chittering calls,

but another part of me was trying hard not to believe own senses.

Suddenly there was a heavy clanging noise over Something had clambered up onto the roof of the bu was moving slowly toward the open hatch. For a ter moment, we all looked up.

I stood in the dark, mildewy-smelling bus, at the fo the ladder. The thing peered through the hole in the and then its head seemed to split, peeling open like the als of a strang, poisonous flower, revealing a huge, hu mouth filled with hundreds of teeth. I let out a high scr like every terrified girl in every horror movie. I'd see kinds of monster flicks and slashers, but I'd never really derstood the girl in the horror movie before.

Then Steve was in front of me, shoving me out o way, squaring up with the bat like he'd face down the w world and take a chunk out of it before he let anythin to us. Next to me, Lucas moved closer. He reached fo hand, and without meaning to, I was already reaching b

The thing on the roof bent its awful alien head. I a crawling sensation, like the whole world had come sharp nightmare focus, and all this time I'd only been squ ing at it through a dirty window. The thing threw bac head and let out a long, bone-chilling roar. Then there an answering sound, echoing from someplace off in the tance. The thing on the roof raised its head to listen. A once, it turned and bounded down from the bus and the woods.

We stood frozen in the abrupt silence. Lucas was still beside me. His hand felt warm and comforting in mine. I squeezed it, and he didn't pull it away.

Lucas glanced at me, his eyes very wide in the dark, and I let go of his hand in a hurry. I was half-sure he'd reached for me by mistake, but I couldn't help thinking how good it had felt to hold on to him. It seemed ridiculous that three hours ago, I'd been worrying about the distance between Indiana and California, when the universe was so impossibly big.

CHAPTER FIFTEEN

The sky was completely dark now, scattered with all the stars I couldn't see in San Diego. The Milky Way stretched over us, delicate and alien. The woods seemed to drift by. Every tree and branch stood out sharply for a second and was gone again almost as soon as we passed it.

I followed the others through the thick underbrush of the woods, and then along the railroad tracks, like I was walking in a dream. We followed the sound of the monsters, a roaring through the trees like an angry wind.

I'd always been ready for any big adventure, perfectly happy to be dragged along with my dad on his schemes and scams and projects. You had to move fast to keep up with him. I'd thought that made me ready for anything. Everything Lucas had told me in the arcade came rushing back: The mysterious other world, the monsters, the secret lab. Will getting lost in a dangerous, impossible place. The Mage. Now the story was all happening around me, and I didn't know where it was going or how it would end. I had to just keep moving my feet and roll with whatever happened next.

When the sound came again, the others all started after it, plunging away from the tracks into the woods. After a second, I followed them.

. . .

The lab was a huge concrete building like a hospital, except the whole place, including a gatehouse, was behind a high fence with barbed wire along the top. We stood up on the wooded hill above it, looking down at the road. A beat-up old car was sitting at the gate with its lights on. It seemed like a strange thing to find when the lab was closed and the whole place was dark. A slender girl and a shaggy-haired boy had gotten out of the car and were staring up at the fence. They looked like they were probably in high school.

When we stepped out of the trees, the two of them whipped around like they were on high alert, then stood staring in surprise. *"Steve?"*

As soon as we came crunching out of the woods and down to the gatehouse, it was obvious that everyone knew everyone else, but no one had expected to find the others here. The shaggy-haired boy turned out to be Will's brother, Jonathan, and the girl was Mike's sister, Nancy, and they'd come out to the lab to check on Will. As they all discussed what was going on, I learned that Will and Mike were supposedly inside the lab and very much in danger. With the gate locked, though, there was no way to get inside. During the day, there was probably a guy in a wheelie chair sitting in the little gatehouse to buzz people in, but now it was empty. Everything was very quiet.

We stood in the middle of the road while Dustin and Will's brother messed around in the gatehouse, trying to figure out how to open the gate.

We were still just standing there when all the lights came on at once and the gate slid open. Jonathan and the girl got back in their car and drove into the compound to look for Will. The rest of us waited.

While we did, Lucas told me about Will and the lab, how they were monitoring him after the time he'd spent lost in the otherworld. We didn't talk about the junkyard, but I kept remembering the awful, gaping mouth studded with teeth. I kept remembering how it had felt to hold Lucas's hand.

We were still in the middle of the road, trying to figure out what to do next, when suddenly a blaze of headlights came rushing toward us, and we all scattered out of the way. We stood watching as the lights got closer and Jonathan's car came roaring past us up the drive, followed by a hulking Blazer with a Hawkins Police Department shield painted on the side. The Blazer skidded to a stop in front of us, and the driver leaned across to the passenger-side window.

He was a big burly man with a lot of stubble. "Let's go."

I'd been warned my whole life not to get into cars with strangers, but I figured maybe that didn't count if it was a police car, and anyway, there was nothing left to do.

The drive from the lab was very quiet. None of us talked about it, but I knew from the way the cop was staring into the dark that something terrible had happened. The look on his face was too grim to mean anything else. I could still smell the rancid stink of the monsters in the junkyard, —or maybe the smell was on him, too, seeping into everything.

We drove along a narrow two-lane road that wound through the trees. The house was tucked deep in the woods, even farther outside of town than ours. It was small and shabby, with a sagging porch, not much different from any of the little one-story bungalows I'd lived in with my mom back in California.

When we pulled up to the house, the other car was already there, and I finally got a good look at everyone else. Mike and Will had been at the lab, along with Will's mom. The big, grim-faced man was named Hopper, and he was the chief of police. The girl we'd met at the gatehouse was Nancy Wheeler, and she was Mike's sister.

I had about a thousand questions, but I mostly stayed quiet. The only thing I knew for sure was that I'd thought our standoff in the junkyard was the strangest thing that

ould happen all night—maybe the strangest thing that
ould happen in my whole life—but instead I'd stumbled
back into the middle of something even bigger and more
bizarre. There was no *Previously, on . . .* segment or voice-
over to catch me up. The story was happening, and had been
for a while. They were all part of it—not just Steve or the
boys, but everyone. Will's mom and brother, Mike's sister,
Hopper. Lucas and Dustin didn't seem even a little surprised
to find them there.

We piled out of the cars and went inside. I'd expected
a cozy, messy atmosphere, run-down maybe, but normal.
When we stepped inside, though, the whole place looked
deranged. It was full of drawings, hundreds of them, taped
over the floor and the walls. Each one was part of a bigger whole, branching and forking like veins under the skin
of something huge.

They laid Will on the couch, but he was completely
conked out. I still wasn't sure what was wrong with him. All
they'd told us was that they'd had to break out of Hawkins
Lab, which was abandoned now and full of monsters. They
were keeping Will sedated, which had something to do with
that and the hungry, slinking monsters we'd seen in the
backyard.

As we sat at the kitchen table, I started to piece together
the story from things the boys were saying, but the picture
was getting was wild. They kept calling the animals in the
backyard something that, at first, sounded like *demon-dogs*.

But as they kept talking, I realized they were say
demodog. The place Will had gotten lost in was where
monsters came from, and even though he was back n
something that lived there had gotten inside his head.
his body. The difference was hard to figure out. Mike
Dustin called it the Mind Flayer, but the important part
that it had found a way to use Will like a puppet so that t
were always connected. It would be able to find him. An
it could find him, it could find us.

That was why they were keeping him full of some k
of heavy-duty tranquilizer, with shots in his arm an
backup syringe loaded with an extra dose: so the thing
had set up shop in his brain wouldn't have a chance to l
out through his eyes and see us.

It was awful to see how hard Will's mom had worked
to keep him safe, and even though I'd never thought he
scary before, the thing inside him had made him into sor
thing terrible. He was part of the monster now, and still,
was ready to do anything to save him.

We sat and waited in the dark house, while out in
shed his family was doing everything they could to le
how to stop the Mind Flayer before it found us.

It was no good, though. When Hopper came cha
ing inside, ordering us to get ready, the dogs were co
ing, I wanted to let myself believe they could protect
from whatever happened next. I was a little comforted
how quickly everyone readied themselves. Mike's si
Nancy, was in high school, but she seemed way differ

from the high school girls who went around with Billy. She was preppie and skinny, with large, cautious eyes and dark hair cut in a bob. She looked like the kind of girl who mostly liked Swatch watches and Bonne Bell lip gloss, but when Hopper had handed out weapons, she'd been the one who took the rifle. Her eyes were wide and scared, but she held the gun like she meant it.

I was so afraid that none of it was good enough and we were going to die here in the little brown house, surrounded by monsters. Next to me, Lucas stood with the pocket of his slingshot pulled back. All the weapons seemed small and too ordinary to do much good.

Nancy was standing in front with Steve and Hopper, and she was frightened and delicate like the girls who always screamed the chilling scream in all the stories, but she was fierce, too.

I'd always believed that it wasn't too hard to be strong. That people like my mom just weren't trying hard enough. I knew that girls could be as badass as boys, but before I'd always thought the only way to do it was by being just like them. Nancy didn't seem to be trying to be Steve or Hopper. She was dangerous and brave and frightened all at once. When she lifted her chin and raised the gun to her shoulder, it looked like it belonged there.

We stood in the cramped little living room and waited. The dogs were coming for us, but at least I wasn't facing them alone. For most of my life, I'd been like a balloon tied to a railing somewhere, unprotected. I'd gotten so used to the feeling that it was hard to realize it was gone. The others were all around me now. They didn't even know me, and still, they'd put me in the middle of their circle. They weren't about to just give up and let the world roll over us, the way my mom did.

Outside, the woods had come alive. There were snarls and rustles as the bushes shook below the window. They were coming for us. I wondered what it would feel like to be torn apart by rows and rows of little bristling teeth. It made sense that something would only have a huge, savage mouth like that if it was built to eat everything it touched.

The map of drawings lay in a snaking tangle on the floor, a guide to somewhere terrible and impossible. We'd come close to outsmarting it, but the Mind Flayer had found us anyway.

There wasn't much hope in what we were about to do, but now I thought I understood why they could stand to face it: no matter what happened, they had each other. Most of the time, my mom didn't have anyone. If I was really being honest, most of the time she didn't even have me.

The demodogs were out there, hunting through the woods in a frantic pack. I could almost feel them rushing toward us. And then, without warning, something happened. There was a colossal thump, and a dark shape crashed through the living room window and slid bonelessly to the floor.

Then the door swung open, and it wasn't the army or the State Patrol or a bunch of lab men in hazmat suits.

It was a girl. She stepped into the living room, and I knew, just knew, beyond all question, that this was the girl Lucas had told me about. El, the Mage, had come back.

She stood in front of us, dressed in black with her hair combed back tightly from her face. As soon as Mike saw her, all the misery and the pinched meanness he'd been walking around with seemed to drain out of him. He looked raw and lost and very young. He went to her and hugged her hard, like he knew without question she would hug him back, and it didn't even matter that we were all watching.

The way he reached for her filled me with a weird kind of gladness so unexpected it almost hurt. I had never been that sure about anyone.

CHAPTER
SIXTEEN

When I'd first moved to Hawkins, I'd thought it was small. I'd thought it was the kind of place where nothing ever happened, and the streets were wide and quiet, and the best part about them was they all led out of town. Now we were trying to figure out what to do about a creature from another dimension tearing a hole in the skin of the world.

The situation seemed impossible, but El said she could close the gate. She sounded so sure, so determined, and finally Hopper agreed to take her to the lab. The rest of us stayed behind in the ramshackle Byers house.

Mike was pale and tight-lipped, but I understood his

moods a little better now. I was getting better at knowing how to recognize sadness when someone was being a jerk. It didn't make the way he'd treated me all right, it just made it easier not to take personally.

The grown-ups and the older kids had all gone, except Steve. He was helping Dustin pack up the body of the creature that El had tossed through the window. It turned out that the name Dustin had given them was demodogs, and as helpful as it probably was to get the dead one off the floor, it felt like we should be doing something more important. I was a tomboy and a daredevil and I mostly tried to be brave, but that was nothing compared to how it hard it must have been to be the girl whose job it was to close the gate on a world full of monsters. It was a kind of brave that didn't even seem possible. They'd barely escaped from the lab, and now they were going back in.

The longer we stood around doing nothing, the more restless and wrong it felt, like we were hanging El out to dry. True, she'd ignored me when I'd introduced myself, as if I'd done something wrong, but maybe it didn't matter that much. I tried not to let it get to me.

Steve wasn't about to let us go running off to help her, though. We were all arguing with him about what to do next, when outside there was a low, snarling rumble.

I knew that sound like I knew the sound of my own voice, and I ran to the window. Billy's Camaro came tearing through the trees and roared up the driveway. He'd found us. Found me.

It had been dark for hours by now. Of course Neil and my mom would have gotten home from Terre Haute and freaked out when they found me gone. They'd sent Billy to bring me back. But I honestly had no clue how he'd figured out I was here.

Lucas was right there next to me, leaning against the couch to look out the window. His arm beside mine was warm, but it didn't get rid of the icy feeling creeping down my neck.

When Steve came up behind us and saw what we were looking at, he put his hand on my shoulder. "Don't worry, I'll take care of it."

I didn't try to stop him, but I was plenty worried. He just gave me a reassuring smile and stepped outside into the gravel driveway to meet Billy.

Billy got out of the Camaro, a cigarette jutting from the center of his mouth like always. The cherry glowed a wicked, itchy red, even from the window. Steve was talking to him with a bored look, like nothing about Billy impressed him. Billy was smiling, but I could see from the loose, easy way he moved that he was going to go right through Steve to get to me.

The way they watched each other made me think that maybe it wasn't even about me. Or at least, not all of it. They were looking at each other with the kind of fixed stares you only get when it's personal. Suddenly Billy shoved Steve in the chest, hard enough to knock him backward. Steve went sprawling in the dirt, and Billy raised one booted foot and stomped hard on Steve's ribs. Then he stepped over Steve and up onto the porch.

He came slamming into the house, scanning the living room for me. "Well, well, well."

Then his gaze shifted to find Lucas, and I knew what came next.

"You know what happens when you disobey me!" Billy's face was twisted with rage. "I break things!"

His voice sent a shudder through me. I could almost hear it—the sound of my skateboard deck splintering, the sound of Nate's arm breaking. Billy didn't look like a real person at all anymore but like a grinning, snarling monster. He went straight for Lucas, and I understood that he was going to do something terrible that couldn't be taken back. The moment would stretch on forever. We would never stop living it.

He stalked through the dim, cluttered living room, backing Lucas against the bookcase in the corner, and I waited for the loud, sickening snap.

Instead, Lucas kicked Billy square in the groin.

I was horrified and deeply impressed. My heart was in my throat, sure, but I had wanted to do that for months. When Billy turned on Lucas, he looked ready to murder him. The whole thing felt flat and too bright, like it was happening to someone else.

Suddenly Steve charged back into the house and decked Billy. The punch connected with a dull smack, and Billy threw back his head. He was laughing. I was struck by how

py it was when you hit someone and they just let you
t, laughing like it's everything they ever wanted.

Steve was still trying to talk to Billy, like maybe this could
ust be civil, but Billy wasn't having it. He'd come here to
t. He took a swing at Steve, and then they were shoving
1 other around the kitchen, slamming into the counter.
y reached out, fumbling along the drain board. His hand
1d a plate, and in one fast, fluid motion, he smashed it
the side of Steve's head. Steve staggered, and then Billy
on top of him, swinging his fists in huge, bludgeoning
, beating Steve's face into hamburger.

The boys were screaming for him to stop, but I knew
wouldn't make a difference. The dreamlike feeling was
ng away. Every crumpled drawing and drop of blood was
ing clearer and more real by the second.

'd always known that when Billy lost his temper, it was
rent from how other people got mad. It had still seemed
ivable, though. Manageable. He was out of control, but
u stayed alert, you could weather him like a storm. Now
s horribly sure that if someone didn't do something to
Steve, Billy was going to kill him.

He had Steve pinned to the floor. The others were just
ng in total disbelief, but I'd seen what he could do. Every
I walked around knowing what he'd done to Nate. I'd
what happened when Billy stopped trying to control
self, and now if no one did anything, I was going to see
eone die.

When the demodogs had come, El had shown up at last minute and saved us. There was no one to sweep in save us or work miracles this time. The others might be quainted with monsters, but they hadn't seen one like E

I remembered how it had felt the first time I'd watc the Hargroves in action. Neil standing over Billy with belt in his hand. Neil calling me a stupid little girl for I ing the guts to try to stop him. Making it so clear tha thought I was small and weak and pointless. And knov Neil believed that still wasn't as bad as the way Billy hated me for trying to help him. He was damaged. Bro maybe. And even if he'd been coherent enough to ai with, it wouldn't make a difference. I understood now Neil was in his head, and that meant he was just as dan ous as his father. Worse, because Neil was cruel and frigh ing, but he cared how things looked on the outside. He wanted people to think he was reasonable.

Billy was crazy.

Under Billy's pounding fists, Steve was fading, g limp. His head rocked back.

The others were all watching in shock, like the so had been turned down. The living room was dim and cl trophobic. Everything seemed very close, like being insi cardboard box. Somebody needed to do something.

That backup syringe from the lab was sitting on the ner of a little sewing table. It was full of something colo Whatever it was had been enough to keep Will compl out of commission, and I grabbed it.

There had been times when Billy had seemed exciting, almost fun, but we were so far beyond that now. I uncapped the syringe, already reeling at what I was about to do.

It felt like I'd spent my whole life thinking about how things worked, figuring out the rules for locks and people, memorizing my escape routes. Billy had never been a problem that was solvable; he was just something I had to live through. Tonight, though, I was done with monsters.

The syringe felt small and weightless in my hand, the kind of thing that was more dangerous than it looked. The needle was sharp, just waiting to end up somewhere.

Holding it like a knife, I shouldered my way between the boys. I crossed the floor in two quick strides and jammed the syringe into the side of Billy's neck.

There was a smooth, bottomless feeling when the needle slid into the skin. I'd been expecting some kind of resistance, but there wasn't any. I clenched my jaw and pressed the plunger. For a horrible second, I was sure whatever was in the syringe wouldn't be strong enough. Billy was too angry and too ferocious to stop. He would whip around and grab me by the throat and squeeze till I was dead.

Then he froze, and his eyes slid out of focus. He got to his feet and turned to face me. The syringe was sticking out of the side of his neck, and he went to pull it out, but it was too late.

"What the hell is this?" His face was dumbfounded and slack.

He staggered and fell back, limp and boneless, like he was tumbling into a swimming pool. He was laughing in a slow, drunk way, trying to look at me, but his eyes kept fluttering closed. He was trying to fight it, but the drug was in his blood now.

Steve's bat was leaning against the wall. It looked like a weapon out of a Texas chain saw torture shed, covered in a spiky layer of nails, perfect for killing monsters. When I grabbed it up and hefted in my hands, it felt serious—heavier than I'd expected.

I stood over him with the bat, watching a blurry comprehension come into his eyes.

He stared up at me, trying to focus, and for a second, I wondered if he was even seeing me.

After being abducted, Will had turned into something terrible and frightening, but even with the Mind Flayer working through him, he was trying not to let it. His mom was terrified pretty much all the time, but she was ready to fight for him, no matter how scary he was, no matter how hard it got or how dangerous. He'd almost gotten us killed, but you couldn't even blame him, because he didn't ask for this. He was trying so hard to stop it.

Billy lay on the floor at my feet, moving his arms in useless little jerks, like they weighed too much to lift.

I gestured with the bat. "From here on out, you leave me and my friends alone. Do you understand?"

Billy was trying to sit up. He looked up at me, dazed and resentful. "Screw you."

I slammed the bat down as hard as I could. The nails bit into the floor half an inch from the crotch of his jeans. "Say you understand!"

It came to me that we would never be here in this room, in this awful, impossible moment, ever again. It was a miracle. A gift. And I needed to make it count.

"Say it!" I shouted, holding the bat like I was standing over home plate.

I couldn't protect the girls who went around with him. They were drawn to him in their own whacked-out ways, for their own reasons. Maybe it was what they wanted—or what they thought they wanted. I'd been drawn to him too, and it wasn't what I wanted, but it was what I thought that I deserved. Or else, maybe I'd just believed it was all there was. Maybe that was how it was for everyone.

When I stood over him with the bat, I had a fierce, glowing feeling like a comic-book hero: righteous. I was doing this for the girls he messed around with, for the way he grabbed and sneered and talked about them later with his friends. For my mom, who, no matter how many times she got burned, was always ready to believe that the worst, most despicable parts of people didn't define them. For myself, because I understood that things were messed up and dysfunctional and just rolled with it anyway since I'd spent so long believing there were no other options.

The bat was heavy in my hands, but it belonged there.

The universe was very big. I mean, there were places where the fabric of reality opened onto whole other worlds!

The boys were all standing behind me, huddled against the wall. I bent down and yanked the keys from Billy's pocket. I had nothing but options.

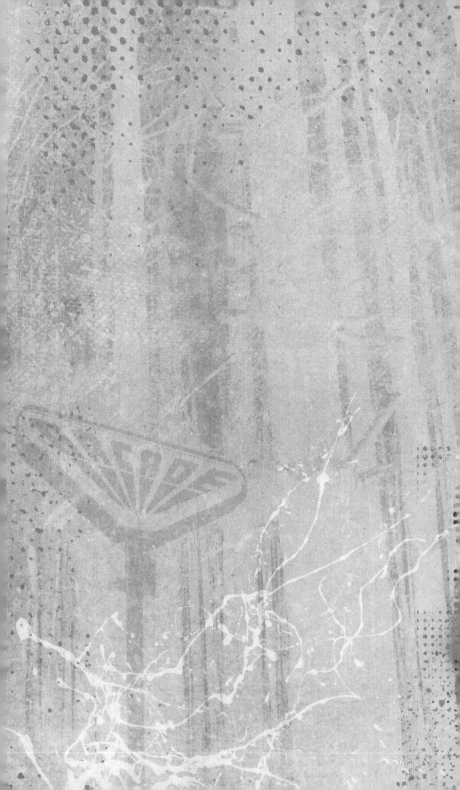

CHAPTER SEVENTEEN

A month before this, I wouldn't have been caught dead getting ready for the Snow Ball. The whole time I'd been in California, I never went to a dance. At least, none except for the last week of day camp in fifth grade, when they forced us to do square dancing.

Now I was standing in front of the bathroom sink, in my good sweater and my salmon-colored pants, getting ready for the winter dance at Hawkins Middle School.

My mom stood behind me, fixing my hair. I forced myself to hold still, trying to get used to the weird, cautious feeling of her fingers in my hair. She tugged gently, braiding the front of my hair back from my face. I watched us in the mirror. The strangeness of having her so close made me rest-less and twitchy.

"Ow!" I said, even though it didn't hurt that much.

When she'd pinned the braid in place with a barrette, she clasped her hands and stepped back to inspect my sweater. "Are you sure you wouldn't rather wear a dress?"

"No, this is good."

She frowned a little. "Won't all the other girls be in dresses?"

"I don't know. Probably?"

She looked sort of surprised by that, but she smiled. "Always my little rebel, aren't you, marching to your own drum."

I grinned, even though I wanted to roll my eyes over being called little. "Yep."

When she was done giving me the once-over, she put an arm around my shoulders and stood next to me in front of the mirror. Our reflections were similar, freckled and red-headed, but her hair was a shade or two darker. I'd always just assumed that I was more like my dad, but so much of me was my mom. She looked wistful and a little worried, but proud, too. She looked happy.

With a distracted sigh, she turned to me and tapped a thumb against my mouth. "What about some lipstick? Just a little dab?"

I made my eyelids heavy and gave her a long look. "Don't push it."

But I could feel myself smiling.

I wasn't going to magically turn into her ideal daughter, but I wasn't disappointing, either. It felt weird to be dressed up, trying to look pretty just for a dance, but it wasn't the same as giving up the person I was the rest of the time. I was still me. I would always be myself, even with my fancy braid and my sweater and my mom's fingers in my hair.

She was always going to be my mom, even when she made herself small and gave away all her time and attention to guys like Neil. She would keep choosing him, making dinner and excuses for him, and there was nothing I could do to fix it. I couldn't change the men she picked and the things she put up with, but I could love her without feeling obligated to make the same choices.

Deciding to back away from the monster was easier, knowing that I wasn't alone here in Hawkins. That there were a whole lot of people who would show up and fight for each other. If I trusted them and if I let them, maybe they'd show up for me, too.

When I glanced over my shoulder, Billy was standing in the doorway, watching me and my mom. Since that night at the Byers house, he'd been careful to stay out of my way. There was still a dark fury in his face sometimes, when I took the time to look for it. He hadn't come after me or any of my friends, but I knew I wouldn't be safe from him forever. He was the same person he'd always been, and that empty, glittering rage still flashed across his face at random times. I thought I saw it in the center of his pupils, blacker and emptier than before. I needed to be careful.

For a long, uneasy moment, we looked at each other, but neither of us said anything. After a second, he turned and disappeared down the hall.

There had been times in my life when he was the coolest, most exciting thing that had happened to me, and times when he'd been the worst. Now, though, I thought I could just settle in and live with him until I didn't have to anymore. Since coming to Hawkins, I'd seen things so wild and fantastical that the hugeness of it made Billy seem smaller somehow. Less real.

After I'd jabbed him with the needle, we hadn't stuck around. He was passed out on the floor, and it was crucial to help El and Hopper in whatever way we could. With Steve out of commission after Billy had bounced his head off the floor, there'd been no one to stop us.

I'd driven us all out to a pumpkin field in the Camaro and then followed the others underground into a winding network of tunnels. Not the place where Will had disappeared to, but a dark, sprawling nest that the monsters had made for themselves in our world.

We'd found the demodogs and drawn their attention until El could do whatever big, dangerous miracle it took to close the gate. We'd done it because we needed to. Because El was some kind of magician or a mutant—a real superhero, maybe—but she was still just one person. She had the power to save us from the monsters, but she didn't have to do it alone, and when the whole world was on the line, her friends were ready to do whatever it took to help her.

• • •

At school, the halls were decorated with posters and banners for the dance, painted in icy blues and silvers. The gym was transformed, dripping with tinsel and streamers, with a disco ball and a punch bowl. Nancy Wheeler stood behind a folding table, handing out refreshments, while Jonathan took photos against a marbled backdrop. The whole place was full of boys in khakis and girls with feathered hair and dresses filled out with shoulder pads.

Lucas and Mike were both looking awkward and uncomfortable in collared shirts and sport coats. Most of the other boys were dressed pretty much the same, but Dustin was wearing a bow tie and had combed his hair into a huge, curly pompadour. He looked ridiculous, but comforting and familiar, too. The fact that he was wearing high-top sneakers with his dress slacks made me feel less like an idiot in a costume and more like I was just trying on a new version of myself. If it didn't fit, I could still take it back.

The version of me who wore a shiny barrette in her hair and let her mom touch her face didn't feel so terrible, though. Maybe I would keep it.

A slow song came on. Lucas was looking at me with kind, steady eyes. Usually he was unflinchingly direct, but tonight he was having a hard time getting the words out. He kept making it halfway through a sentence, then picking a different one and starting over. After I got tired of watching him stammer and squirm, I grabbed his hand and tugged him onto the dance floor.

It was easier to understand the hugeness of all the secrets he'd had to keep from me now, and to appreciate how hard he'd tried to explain them anyway. When I thought back to that night, it seemed almost like something I'd imagined, like remembering a dream. The clearest parts were also the most impossible—hiding from the demodogs in a junkyard, arguing over how to close the gate on the Mind Flayer. Stabbing Billy with a syringe full of drugs. I had taken his keys. I had *driven his car*. We'd all gone underground together in a last-ditch effort to keep the horde of demodogs away from El long enough for her to save the world.

Certain things were burned into my mind so clearly I could still see their outlines when I shut my eyes, but I didn't know if there was any way I'd ever be able to say them out loud to someone who didn't already know.

Now here I was, with Lucas's hands on my waist, his face inches from mine. I darted forward and kissed him. It was fast and awkward, but his mouth was warm and the feeling of us there together in the middle of the gym was exactly what I wanted. I leaned against him and rested my head on his shoulder.

When the Mage showed up, no one really seemed to notice her. She stood hesitantly at the edge of the dance floor, and I had to turn and crane my neck for another look.

She'd come to the house in the woods looking wild and edgy, like Joan Jett or Siouxsie Sioux, but that version of her was long gone. Now she looked clean and young and shy. Like a girl. Just any ordinary girl, with lip gloss and soft, tousled curls. Her dress was grown-up and a little too big, like it had belonged to someone else.

Mike went to El, and his shoulders were tense, but his face was earnest and unguarded. The way he looked at her was so tender. Sure, he was still way too serious and he could be moody as hell, but he'd been nicer to me lately. I didn't really know who she was—what she wished for or why she liked him. But she did. Maybe all that really mattered was that she did.

Lucas was watching me as we swayed to the music, bending closer. When he kissed me, it was gentler and less awkward this time, and I felt my cheeks go a hot, flaming red, but I didn't care. I was there in Hawkins, with my hands on Lucas's shoulders in the middle of the dance floor, and for once, I was totally sure I belonged there.

ACKNOWLEDGMENTS

My gratitude belongs to:

My agent, Sarah Davies, who is wise, kind, sensible, and tireless. It's been ten years and I still count on you every step of the way.

My publisher, Michelle Nagler, for her vision, encouragement, and willingness to follow me down rabbit holes, and my intrepid editors, Rachel Poloski and Sara Sargent. Rachel got me started and Sara saw me through.

Krista Marino, for her continual faith in me and for remembering everything I like.

The whole *Stranger Things* team, for answering questions, sharing my love of the '80s, being generally and genuinely delightful, and creating an extraordinary world full of kind boys, fearsome monsters, and dangerous girls and then letting me dabble around in it.

And to David, who made this book possible, and Veronica, who sometimes made it impossible but in the most miraculous way. I love you both.

JUNE 8, 1984

I run so fast the lockers blur. Stitches in my abruptly altered dress pop as I pass couples who've cut out of the festivities in favor of making out in the darkened senior hallway. Their egregious kissing would usually be enough to get me to turn around and seek an alternate route, but right now it's just gross background noise.

This feels like a nightmare I've had a thousand times—running through the halls of Hawkins High School. But even in my most extreme dream scenarios, I've never had this little hair. I've never been wearing this much makeup. And prom night has *never* been thrown into the mix by my subconscious.

I'm nearly at the end of senior hall. No turning back now.

I'm headed into the belly of the high school beast—which is the weirdest part of all, because in my dreams I'm always trying to break out of this place. I would never, ever voluntarily break *in*.

"Stop right there, Miss Buckley!" shouts a voice, pinched and petty and adult-sounding. One of the incensed mom chaperones.

"Hey! Back here! Now!" That gravelly command was definitely issued by Chief Hopper.

It's not a real rebellion unless you're in trouble with authority—right?

I wonder how much trouble I could get in for crashing prom and causing some moderate property damage on the way in. Suspension? Expulsion? Would the irate parents of Hawkins High students press charges for what I just did in the parking lot?

I run faster.

Rounding the corner, I pass the concessions that line the hallway outside the gym. About a dozen people are mingling and grazing on platters of cookies and chips and trying to figure out exactly how spiked the punch is.

"Robin!" The sound of my name echoes down the hall. Dash is the one shouting it now. Dash, who I used to think was my friend.

I need to slow him—and all of my detractors—down. So I make a *tiny* detour, barreling into the table that holds about seventy gallons of (judging by the smell, extremely spiked) punch. It pours out in a cascade and I leap forward, avoiding the worst of the spill as everyone else screams and gets their prom attire coated in sticky chemical sugar.

The big double doors of the gym are in sight now. From inside, I can hear the hard-driving heartbeat of a New Wave hit. Is Tammy Thompson already dancing? What will she think when she sees me burst in, wild and reckless and trailed by local law enforcement?

What will she say when I tell her how I feel?

No more time for hypotheticals.

I throw the double doors open. The prom greets me with wild synthesizers and the smells of sweat and AquaNet.

"Hey, Tam," I whisper, practicing for the big moment of terrifying honesty when I show her how I've felt all year, and in doing so simultaneously turn this rebellion all the way up to eleven. "Do you want to dance?"

SEPTEMBER 6, 1983

The first history class of the year hasn't even started, and I know exactly how it's going to unfold, minute by minute, period by period. I have the entire academic year pegged. At least, I swear I do, until Tammy Thompson walks in.

Something about her is different.

Maybe it's her hair. It used to be pin-straight and red. Now it's short, tousled, and redder. It could be her smile. In freshman year, she was semi-popular and at least semi-fine-with-it, but now we're sophomores and she's got a grin that says she's determined to win friends and influence prom queen elections. (Not that we can go to prom as sophomores, unless an upperclassman invites us, an event so rare and special that people in this school talk about it like it's a meteor sighting.)

Maybe it's the fact that when I see her, music infiltrates my brain.

Soft, obnoxious music.

Wait. My brain would *never* play Hall and Oates. I twist around in my seat and realize that Ned Wright is in the back of the room with a boombox perched on his shoulder. He's turned it down so Miss Click—sitting at her desk, ignoring us like a pro, acting like we don't exist until the bell rings—won't confiscate it. When class starts, he'll slide it under his desk and use it as a footrest. (He's been doing this since eighth grade. He's also a pro.) But for right now, Tammy Thompson is strolling across the room on a cloud of "Kiss on My List" and raspberry-scented . . . something. Lotion? Shampoo? Whatever it is, it reminds me of the scratch-and-sniff stickers I collected with a fervor back in middle school.

She slides into a seat, and her friends greet her in high-pitched flutters.

"Oh my gosh, your hair."

"How was the beach, Tam?"

Tam?

Maybe that's the difference—she's got a new nickname to go with her fresh haircut and enhanced smiling capabilities. "Tam," I whisper, quietly enough that nobody can hear me under the how-was-your-summer uproar.

Miss Click looks up. Ominously.

One minute until class starts. If I was a run-of-the-mill

nerd, like I'm pretending to be, I would have a stack of pristine, unsullied white notebook pages ready to go. I would have already done a few chapters of the reading to get a jump start. My pencils would all have perfect, identical, weapons-grade points.

As it is, I plunge down at the last minute and rummage in my bag, looking for my history textbook and anything that will leave a mark on paper. There's a graveyard of gum on the underside of the desk. And the perm I let Kate talk me into right at the end of summer—the perm that made my scalp tingle for a week and still makes my head smell perpetually like overcooked eggs—means my hair is big enough that I have to be extra careful how much space I leave for clearance.

I almost hit my head on the underside of the desk when I hear her start to sing.

Tammy's voice rises over . . . Hall's? Oates's? It's bold and sweet and, yes, she uses vibrato as generously as I peanut butter my sandwiches, but the point is, she's not afraid. Everyone can hear her. I come back up from my deep dive into my backpack and look around at our classmates, but nobody seems to care that Tam is now singing her heart out in the middle of the room with thirty seconds to go until class starts. And she doesn't seem to care if anyone is watching.

What does *that* feel like?

I spin my pencil, feeling every one of the six edges on my finger.

Then the bell rings, Miss Click stands up, and everything slides back into place, exactly the way I thought it would be.

Including when Steve Harrington shows up three and a half minutes late, looking lost, probably because his hair flopped into his eyes and he couldn't see any of the classroom numbers. How does he get anywhere with that hair? It looks even bigger than it did last year.

"Hey, people," he says.

Everyone laughs like the part in a sitcom where the audience guffaws at the main character's not-particularly-funny motto. They know they don't have to do that in real life, right? Even Miss Click beams at him like his hair somehow cured cancer. That's an extreme and rarefied level of popularity, where even the teachers don't glare at you because you're simply too socially precious.

Steve jams himself into the desk next to Tam.

She turns the color of a fresh raspberry.

This whole thing is so ridiculous that my brain glitches and my fingers stop working and my pencil drops to the linoleum with a hard clatter. When I go to pick it up, it's just out of reach. I duck, I grasp, but I can't quite get it. When I finally do, I feel so triumphant that I come up way too fast and knock my head on the underside of the desk. Aka the gum graveyard. My head clangs hard, and my frizzed-out perm touches a dozen ancient pieces of gum at once. They're so hardened that they don't stick to me.

Which is good. And also horrifying.

"Robin, do you need to go to the nurse's office?" Miss Click asks with a pitying look as I resurface. Her concern is touching.

"Unless the nurse has a time machine that will take me back exactly one class period, no."

"All right, then," she says, launching into her first-class-of-the-year monologue.

At least the attention of my classmates doesn't last long. And Tam doesn't even seem to notice my disgrace. (Not that I want her to.) But it bothers me, just a tiny bit, that the reason she *doesn't* notice me is that she's too busy humming "Kiss on My List" while she stares at Steve Harrington.

SEPTEMBER 7, 1983

I wanted to make it through my entire schedule before declaring this outright, but I am truly not impressed with sophomore year.

"It's like all of the teachers just gave up," I say. "Like they collectively decided that this year is the dead zone of our education." I'm one of those weird people who like to actually *learn* while they're in school. At least, I was. Now that I have the creeping, cold, cynical sense that none of our teachers actually want to be here, it's getting harder to care by the minute.

Milton, Kate, and Dash are into school in the intense high-achiever way that they are into everything. At the beginning of our first band practice, when I suggest that sophomore year doesn't really count, they seem taken aback. Milton actually gasps.

Kate frowns and shuffles through her music and drill charts (which she doesn't need, because she's had everything memorized for months). She's shorter than I am—well, most of the girls in our grade are shorter than I am, so I'm not sure if that's a helpful description. Kate is five foot zero and zero-tenths, although she likes to say that her perm adds at least two inches. "If our teachers don't care about our education, we're going to have to care twice as hard."

That's Kate. She fights for everything, including battling her way to first chair of the trumpet section as a sophomore.

"We're all reaching the point where we're pretty much smarter than our teachers, anyway," Dash adds with a smirk.

Dash doesn't work nearly as hard as Kate. Dash—short for Dashiell James Montague, Jr.—sits in the front row of every class but doesn't take notes, claiming that he retains everything. Then he skips showering on the day of the test, shoves everything into his head, and gets an A. He says he's enamored of learning, but he only has eyes for his GPA. Plus, he doesn't seem to notice that his lack of showering on test day throws off everyone in a ten-foot radius, which really isn't fair to the people around him who are trying to write coherent five-paragraph essays.

You know the type.

"Seriously, though, I think all four of us are smarter than ninety percent of the teachers in this school," Dash asserts.

"You're not smart enough to realize that I can hear you," Miss Genovese declares without looking up from her sheet music.

"She's got scary-good hearing," Milton whispers.

"Yes. Yes, I do," Miss Genovese agrees. "That's why I'm the band teacher. I can hear every wrong note you play, too," she announces to the group in general. "And it pains me. Your reedy squeaks haunt my dreams."

She goes over to help Ryan Miller in the percussion section with his quads. Dash waves at us all to come closer. I sniff cautiously. His auburn hair looks clean, and he's giving off the scent of pine soap. No tests imminent. I scooch my chair closer. "Teachers are just scary in general," he whispers. "I don't think they're here to teach us. I think they're here to feed off our innate potential."

"Like vampires?" Milton asks. He's taking this way too seriously. But Milton is very, very serious. And nervous. I'd worry about him, but he worries so much it's probably redundant.

"Think about it. They're not really that bright, they move slowly through the halls, they need our brains to survive. They're clearly zombies."

Milton and I groan. Kate gives a nervous giggle.

Dash has been on a horror movie kick since fifth grade, when he realized it set him apart from kids who still slept with night-lights. The gleeful sense of superiority never quite faded. If it eats flesh, drinks blood, or lurks in the shadows, Dash is on board. This year we watched *Evil Dead* over the summer. A lot. He got a top-of-the-line VCR for his last birthday—yes, his *own* VCR, which is ridiculous even by rich-people standards—and he kept inviting everyone over for viewing parties, but no matter what tape he boasted about having, we always ended up watching *Evil Dead*.

I stopped going sometime in August, pretending that my parents needed me to help out more at home. The truth was, I couldn't handle watching Kate and Dash inch closer and closer to each other on the couch, the whole time acting like they didn't know their thighs were on a collision course.

That's another thing about sophomore year.

In middle school, crushes were talked about exclusively on the bus and during sleepovers, and dating was a novelty. In freshman year, relationships became inevitable. This year, things have ramped up to a complete frenzy. We're less than a week in, and there have already been a slew of hallway make-outs, dramatic breakups, and declarations of undying love. The situation is amped up in marching band because we start practices halfway through the summer.

I give the room a quick scan. At least half of the girls in the band room are wearing jewelry inscribed with the names of their boyfriends, who are also in band. (Band nerds date band nerds: it's the law of the land.) When a couple makes it official, the boy gives the girl a gold anklet with both of their names on a gold nameplate charm. But most of the girls don't think that anyone can see the evidence of their boyfriends' devotion, so they buy longer gold chains and wear the nameplate charms around their necks.

I've been waiting for the day when Dash finally gives one to Kate. (Really, Kate's been waiting for that day, and I've been waiting by proxy.) Even right now, at this very moment, Kate and Dash are sending each other looks in some kind of Morse code.

Dash's eyelashes: *Let's make out later.*

Kate's eyelashes: *Maybe!*

Dash's eyelashes: *Really?!?!*

Kate's eyelashes: *I already said maybe. I'm first chair, practice is about to start, you're distracting me.*

Dash's eyelashes: *But you're so pretty.*

Kate's eyelashes: *Really?!?!*

I don't know how much of this I can tolerate.

All Kate wants to talk about now is boys in general, and Dash specifically. It's bad enough when popular girls like Tammy Thompson completely lose track of their own brains over hapless hair piles like Steve Harrington.

Which brings me back around to the zombie conversation. "If our teachers are undead, they're also undernourished. Have you noticed how hungry they look? Our brains aren't giving them much sustenance. Maybe we aren't as smart as we think we are. Maybe it's because everyone's too obsessed with *dating stuff* all of a sudden."

Hint. Hint.

Kate just gives another nervous laugh and turns back to her trumpet, practicing her fingering for one of the many John Philip Sousa marches Miss Genovese is always inflicting on us.

I scared her off, but I don't feel better about it.

"All right," Miss Genovese says. "Time to get your squads for the 1983 marching band season in order! You have three minutes to name yourselves, and not a second longer. Please don't ask me how long it's been. There is a clock above the door."

Groups of four huddle together—except for ours, which is already gathered. I'm the only French horn in marching band. Well, technically I only play the French horn in concert band. In marching band it's a mellophone, which is played in exactly the same way but is slightly flattened instead of round, so I can carry it around for months on end. Freshman year, Miss Genovese tacked me onto a squad with three trumpet players, which makes sense, I guess, because the mellophone looks like a trumpet with bonus squiggles in the middle section. Since that moment, the four of us have been socially fused. Kate likes to say we're an atom, because that's the kind of endearingly nerdy metaphor she goes in for.

But the truth is, even with all the time we've spent together in the band room and on the field, on the bus and at games, I'm not *quite* as fused as the rest of the group. On some level—the subatomic one, I guess—I get the sense that I don't quite fit in with most of the band kids. That no matter how much time I spend with them, I'll never be *one* of them. And that can be scary because at Hawkins High, standing out is pretty much a death sentence unless you're popular.

"All right," Dash says, snapping me back into the moment. "Sophomore year squad name. Go."

"We're going to be Odd Squad again, right?" Milton asks. "We already voted on it last year. I think we should keep it that way, for continuity, and also because coming up with a new name is going to be an ordeal." Milton is the only junior in our group, and while his quiet, nervous nature keeps him from acting like the de facto leader, Kate and Dash tend to listen when he speaks up like this.

"I love Odd Squad!" Kate says.

"Odd Squad it is," Dash adds.

I nod. Not that they were waiting for my vote.

We spend the next two minutes in silence. Kate and Dash have moved on from eye-flirting to ankle-flirting. (I've seen Dash's feet: gross.) I concentrate on getting ready to play for the first official practice of the year. I have the pieces memorized, but that's only half the battle with my instrument. Let's be honest: it's murder compared to most of the instruments in this room. It's an elaborate contraption of metal tubes that seems to exist solely to bleat out a squeak at exactly the wrong moment. I chose it back in elementary school because no one else wanted to play it. I don't exactly regret my choice—but I wish someone had told me how much time I'd spend emptying a spit valve.

We figured out our squad name too fast. We still have two minutes left. Two minutes of nothing. Now, thanks to Miss Genovese's little reminder about the existence of the clock, all I can seem to do is listen to it. It's one of those big, round black-and-white ones with a second hand that audibly clicks the moments of your life away.

Click. Click. Click.

Three more seconds gone.

I catch Miss Genovese staring at the exit door in the back. I've seen her run for the teachers' parking lot the second school ends to light up one of her beloved menthols. I've smelled the smoke stubbornly clinging to her hair after lunch. She leaves the room like there's a fire at her heels—just enough time for a quick one.

Our teachers don't want to be here. My classmates only care about rubbing up against each other. I'm supposed to get through three more years of this, how?

Right when I'm thinking about standing up and strolling out the door, Sheena Rollins, who plays oboe, does that exact thing. Or at least she tries. When she gets close, one of the jerkwads in the percussion section bars her way.

If I'm worried about not quite belonging, Sheena Rollins is the poster child for aggressively not fitting in. She's in the class ahead of me, so it feels like I've had a front-row seat for the year-by-year increase in bullying as she got overtly stranger. Her wardrobe is part of it. She wears white from head to toe: sometimes it's white overalls and a white tiara, and sometimes it's a puffy white miniskirt and an oversize flowing shirt. None of it follows the unspoken code of what everybody else is wearing. And most of the time, it looks like Sheena sewed at least part of the outfit herself. (Another point of bullying for my brand-obsessed peers.) Today she's in a white fifties-style dress with tiny black dots, and a white cloth headband.

"Hey, Sheena," someone says. "What do you think you're doing? Teacher's not here to give out passes. Sit your polka-dotted ass down."

Sheena pushes her lips together, but she doesn't sling a comeback. She doesn't say a word.

Here's the other thing about Sheena Rollins: I remember her from elementary school as a soft-spoken kid, but I haven't heard her speak a word since seventh grade. She even plays the oboe so quietly that Miss Genovese is constantly telling her to "blow harder." (Which doesn't exactly help when it comes to vulgar joke time.)

"Where are you going?" Craig Whitestone asks, a grin as shitty as cafeteria meat loaf on his face.

Sheena shrugs.

"She's lying," Dash pipes up.

"Dash," I whisper, with an elbow to his side that misses and collides painfully with his trumpet.

"She spends the whole period in the bathroom," Kate informs me, as if that makes it okay that she's been policed by her fellow band members.

"So?" I ask. "Who cares?"

"Band kids don't ditch," Milton reminds us.

"Miss Genovese just ditched," I remind him.

"She's the *teacher*," Kate breathes in a sacred tone. Teachers can do no wrong in her book.

Sheena tries to walk around Craig, but he blocks her. She tries again, head ducked, walking with a little more determination, but Craig grabs her by the ponytail, tugging her back into the room. A few of his fellow jerkwads laugh.

"Hey," I say. "Let her go, you walking spit valve."

"It's their mess," Kate hisses. "Don't get involved."

I know that I shouldn't, on a pure survival level. Which is perhaps the grossest thing of all.

"Hey, Sheena," Craig says. "You're all dressed up with no-where to go. Do you want to dance?"

He nods at his friends, and a few of the band kids start playing sloppily. Sheena jumps on a chair to avoid playing into his stupid joke. Craig just gets down on his knee like he's serenading her, which makes her blush—in a furious way. She jumps off the chair and makes another break for the door, but Craig catches her arm and spins her in a travesty of a dance move. A couple of the big, beefy guys on percussion decide to back Craig up, too. They circle around in front of the double doors so that Sheena really can't leave the music room. They dance in front of her, turning and waggling their butts, and then turning back around and thrusting their hips forward to waggle their . . . other bits.

In case you didn't know this: band kids can be surprisingly lewd. By the time Miss Genovese comes back in, it's like a barnyard crossed with a burlesque, and she can barely rein us in.

"All right." She crosses her skinny little arms. "Who started it?"

I go to point at Craig Whitestone, but Kate grabs my finger. At least half of the class points at Sheena.

"Miss Rollins," Miss Genovese says with a few dry clucks. "That's detention. On the first day. Impressive, really."

Sheena flops back into her chair, looking ready to snap her

oboe into pieces and walk out. But she doesn't. She stays because she has to, and everyone makes her life hell because . . . well, because they do.

A few years ago, most of Sheena's torment came exclusively from the popular kids. But in high school, I've noticed this kind of behavior spreading through the student body, everybody collectively getting better and better at making life miserable for the students who don't fit in.

Maybe I've watched too many of Dash's horror movies, but the truth seems pretty clear.

High school is a monster, and it's eating everyone I know.